DANCE OF LOVE

Polly smiled broadly. She hadn't thought about ballet or Jennifer for nearly half an hour.

"Well, tell me," she asked, looking into Cott's gray eyes. "What did you do after school in L.A.?"

"Oh, wow, it's the beach, you know. That's the center of everything. . . ." His eyes clouded over and Polly suddenly felt uneasy. What if he'd rather be somewhere else?

"But I'll tell you what L.A. *doesn't* have that Mamaroneck does have."

"Oh, what's that?" Polly tried not to sound interested.

"You," he whispered. "And that could make up for everything else."

Bantam Sweet Dreams Romances
Ask your bookseller for the books you have missed

Dance Of Love

Jocelyn Saal

BANTAM BOOKS
TORONTO · NEW YORK · LONDON · SYDNEY

RL 6, IL age 11 and up

DANCE OF LOVE
A Bantam Book / July 1982

ISBN 0-553-20790-3

Published simultaneously in the United States and Canada

---

*Bantam Books are published by Bantam Books, Inc. Its trademark, consisting of
the words ''Bantam Books'' and the portrayal of a rooster, is Registered in U.S.
Patent and Trademark Office and in other countries. Marca Registrada. Bantam
Books, Inc., 666 Fifth Avenue, New York, New York 10103.*

PRINTED IN THE UNITED STATES OF AMERICA

0 9 8 7 6 5 4 3 2 1

Dance of Love

Chapter One

"Polly, come on, will you? It is now *exactly* seven minutes past nine! You're going to be late."

Polly Luria was on her hands and knees searching under her bed for her favorite pair of pink Danskins when her mother called her. She jerked up quickly and hit her head on the baseboard.

"Ouch! Don't get in a sweat, Mom. I'll take my bike." Her eyes made one last survey of the room. Then, shrugging in resignation, she pulled an old pair of frayed black tights from a drawer of her bureau and crammed them into the canvas knapsack that already held her toe shoes, ballet slippers, and leotard.

"They'll just have to do," she muttered, dashing to the mirror to give herself a last inspection. Her dark brown hair was tightly pulled back in a high bun as it always was on Satur-

1

day morning for dance class, and she gave it a pat with one hand as she slung her knapsack over her shoulder and raced out the door of her bedroom.

She took the stairs two at a time and was out the front door in a matter of seconds. "Have a good day, Mom. See you later!" she called as she threw one long leg gracefully over her bike. She always rode a boy's bike—the frames on girls' bikes just weren't big enough for her tall body.

She pedaled swiftly down the drive and swung onto Orchard Street, and from there it was only three short blocks to Halstead Avenue, which led right into Palmer. She passed the neat suburban houses, the trees on their front lawns just starting to change color, and entered the business district that hugged the railroad tracks. In another five minutes she was at the Mamaroneck station.

As she clipped the Citadel lock on her bike to the chain fence, Polly began scanning the crowd on the platform. There she was! Her friend Jennifer, oblivious to the stares of several Saturday commuters, was concentrating hard and staring straight ahead. With one hand on a bench, she was busy practicing some ballet steps. Polly sneaked up behind her and began to speak in an elaborate Russian accent.

"Plees, the turnout, Mademoiselle Taruskin. Where haf your legs been!"

Jennifer whirled sharply, losing her balance, and clutched her throat. "Thanks a lot, Pol. And need I mention that you're late, as usual? I think you're getting worse."

Polly sighed. "Really? My mom says that when she used to bring us to dance class when we were kids, I was always out of the house before she was even dressed. Do you think I'm getting old?" She pulled at the sides of her eyes, smoothing back imaginary wrinkles.

"Not old. It's just that your brain is melting."

Polly laughed and poked her friend in the ribs.

"But even if you *are* getting soft in the head," Jennifer continued, "you sure do a good imitation of Mme Mishkin. For a second I thought she was right behind me. I have these weird feelings like she's after me all the time: 'Plees to loose some weight, mademoiselle. Plees to jump higher!' Boy, it's a drag sometimes, wanting to go into ballet."

"But nice, too," Polly reminded her best friend, reaching over to tuck a strand of ash blond hair back into Jennifer's bun. "And you're built just like a professional dancer, so the odds are with you, remember." Polly sometimes envied Jennifer's neat, almost doll-like form. The kids at Mamaroneck High called them Mutt and Jeff, since they were constantly together and since Polly stood a good six inches above her friend.

"Well, I'm going to need all the odds I can get,

I'll tell you." Jennifer sighed. The two girls moved to the center of the platform with the rest of the crowd. They heard the train whistle, and saw it come around the curve immediately afterward. "This Connecticut College scholarship thing has me worried."

"Yes? Me, too." Polly didn't really want to talk about it much. It was one thing being up for the top prize of the Dance Company Theater School, but it was something else to be in competition for the award with your best friend. Some days she prayed that neither of them would get it and that stuck-up Dawn Sims would win instead. Other days, she wanted Jennifer to have it, since she was firmly convinced that Jennifer was the better dancer and had more of a chance to become a professional. But on still other days, she wanted the scholarship so much she could cry. It would mean two full summers as an apprentice at the Connecticut College master classes and possibly a full college scholarship after that. And most of all, it would mean dancing all day, every day. That was her dream— what she wanted above all else.

She knew, even though she had not really discussed her deepest feelings about the prize with Jennifer for fear of jinxing the whole thing, that her friend felt the same way. They always shared everything—school, ballet, private jokes, summer vacations. Sometimes they talked about what would happen if either of them had a really serious boyfriend, but they decided they would just have to handle that when and if it came along. For now, their friendship was the most important thing. That and ballet.

The train chugged in, and Jennifer and Polly ran up the platform to be in front of the doors of a no-smoking car. There was absolutely nothing worse than to have Mme Mishkin yell in the middle of class, "Who has been sucking on the filthy cigarettes?" That woman had a nose like a German shepherd, and there was no sense in needlessly being accused of smoking. The doors moved apart, and Polly and Jennifer walked into the car with the suburban matrons and rowdy kids, ready for the excitement of a Saturday in Manhattan.

They picked two facing double seats and tossed their gear on one of the unoccupied places. Jennifer stretched back luxuriously and put her feet up on her tote bag. "So, you haven't asked me about the meeting yesterday," she prompted as the train lurched forward and they pulled out of the station.

"Huh-uh. You didn't give me a chance. How's the Harvest Ball entertainment coming?"

"Not bad, actually. We wanted a professional rock band, but we're going to have to make do with our own home-grown bunch from school if we want to have enough left in the treasury for the spring prom. I mean, what's more crucial, after all?" Jennifer's deep blue eyes scanned her friend's face.

Polly shook her head. School politics was the only passion the two girls did not share. Polly couldn't understand why Jennifer was always doing committee work and getting elected to office. High-school politics just left Polly cold, but she never made fun of her friend's enthusiasm.

"What I want to know is, what's to eat?" Polly foraged in her knapsack for the bag of nuts and raisins she always brought along on Saturday mornings. Jennifer leaned over and took a handful.

"You and food, honestly! It's astounding you aren't as big as a hippopotamus. But you know what?"

"What?" Polly asked skeptically, raising one eyebrow.

"I'd like you anyway."

Polly laughed and popped some nuts into her mouth. "Mme Mishkin wouldn't."

"That's for sure. You know how she was pinching Dawn's midriff last week? I thought she was going to tell her she was out of the running for the summer apprenticeship."

"Don't we wish." Polly sighed. Then she frowned, and when she spoke again, her voice was very quiet. "You deserve to get it, Jen. You've worked so hard this past year, and everyone knows you're the best in the class. But do you mind my saying that I'll be just a little jealous if you do get it?"

"You're ridiculous, that's what you are. The scholarship's yours, Polly—it has your name written all over it. But listen," she went on seriously, her delicate, pixieish features becoming very somber, "we'd be real freaks if we weren't slightly envious of one another. So let's not think about it." She thumped her best friend on the knee. "Let's think about getting two fantastic dates for the Harvest Ball and going out with them the rest of this year, next year, and all through college, then marrying them and buying houses right next to each other and having great careers together!" She finished triumphantly in a peal of laughter, and Polly joined her.

"Dream on, Cinderella—dream on!"

They were the last two left in the dressing room. Everyone else was already in the studio warming up, and Polly was frantically pulling on her tights and leotard when she noticed her friend's reflection in the full-length mirror across the room. Jennifer was pressing her hands flat across her chest, and there was a horrified expression on her face.

"What in the name of—? What are you doing to yourself, Jennifer? We'll be late."

"You go ahead. Oh, it's too awful."

"What is?" Polly snapped the elastic of her

left ballet slipper onto her instep and went over to her friend.

"*These!*" She pointed a thumb at each breast in dismay.

"What's wrong with them?"

Jennifer turned a panic-stricken face from the mirror. "I don't know what happened. Here I was going happily through life as a thirty-two A, and then last week I couldn't fit into my bras. I had to spend my allowance on a thirty-two B. It's horrible."

"Why?" Polly laughed, relieved that the problem wasn't serious. "I wish mine would grow."

"Polly, no, you don't!" Jennifer exclaimed hotly. "Ballet dancers can't be big on top, they just can't!"

"That's not true anymore. Even Mr. Balanchine is taking girls with figures these days. I read it in the New York *Times*." She reached over to pull Jennifer away from the mirror. "Now, will you come on."

"Okay." Jennifer sighed. "But I'd still rather be flat-chested. It's so—ethereal, you know?"

Shoving Jennifer ahead of her, Polly steered her into Mme Mishkin's studio, where fifteen other girls were already lined up at the barre. The two of them quickly squeezed into place behind Dawn Sims, who gave them both a withering look as she grudgingly moved up a few inches to make room. "Late again?" she hissed.

"Mesdemoiselles!" The high voice of Natalia

Mishkin pierced the air, and Joey, the ancient accompanist who had been with the school as long as anyone could remember, was so startled he lost his place in the exercise.

"Why for are you never on time, plees, mees?" Natalia Mishkin was a compact, muscular little woman in her late forties. She had danced for Balanchine until age and a hip injury had relegated her to teaching, which, as it happened, she loved even more than performing. She now divided her time between the New York City Ballet School and the Dance Company Theater School where Jennifer and Polly studied, and she was said to have the best eye in the business for new talent. If there was a promising dancer on the scene, Mme Mishkin would see to it that she didn't remain undiscovered for long.

"Sorry, Madame," Jennifer muttered. "It was my fault."

"Always you are not caring enough!" She pounded her long time stick on the floor and stalked down the line of girls, rapping bulging stomachs and bent legs into position. "Thees is no professional." She raised her arms over her head, and Joey began his music for the warm-up at the dance barre.

Polly concentrated hard on keeping her back straight for the pliés as they went through each of the five positions. Then, as her mind began to wander, she stared at Dawn's skinny neck and thought about how much it looked like it belonged on a chicken. If Dawn got that scholarship, she'd just *spit*!

"Now around," Mme Mishkin called out, and the girls' movements changed fluidly, without missing a beat. The routine of the barre was so ingrained Polly didn't have to think about it. Her body knew exactly what it was supposed to do and most days did it flawlessly.

"And on your toes and turn and other side, plees. Polly Lur*ee*ah, you are not with the beat!"

Polly rose up and executed a perfect pirouette to face the opposite direction. It was much nicer to stare at Jennifer's back than at Dawn's. For as long as she could remember, they had stood together in class, perfecting the intricate techniques that one day, if they were very lucky and very talented, might give them the edge on the hundreds of other young dancers in New York who wanted to make it. The only important thing, of course, was that they make it together.

"Let us go to our floorwork, plees, ladies." Mme Mishkin rapped her stick on the floor, and the pianist changed key and mood. Polly scampered into position, sneaking a look at Madame's outfit. She had on black leg warmers over her pink tights and she wore a cutoff black mesh sweater over her plum-colored wrap leotard. Polly thought she looked marvelous. The consummate ballerina, even when she was dressed in sloppy work clothes.

As the girls took their places on the floor, Jennifer managed to squeeze her friend's hand in encouragement—she knew how awful it was to be yelled at by Madame in class. Jennifer didn't have to say a word; her reassuring presence was enough to lift Polly's spirits a bit so she could concentrate singlemindedly on the steps. She watched her image in the mirror and tried to correct the mistakes she noticed. By the end of the hour, she was sweating buckets.

"Head front, bend and up and turn!" Mme Mishkin called the last set of steps for the morning. "Yes, mesdemoiselles, this is nice, this is goot. But you must smile. *Smile!* Show your owdiance you are having wonderful time. Jennifer, plees, you are scowling, not smiling. You look like someone is pinching you, yes? Come, once more. And relax. Take your bows, plees."

The girls had a five-minute break before the next class, and they ran to the dressing room as if they had been released from prison.

"Whew, got some extra lamb's wool?" Polly asked Jennifer. "My toes really hurt." Polly's corns and her badly healed second toe, which she'd broken two summers ago on a wild roller skating foray, were forever giving her problems.

Jennifer handed her a wad of lamb's wool, which Polly began arranging over her sore toes. "When do you think she'll announce—?" Jennifer quickly shut her mouth as Dawn came tripping over to their bench, sat down next to Polly, and began putting on her toe shoes.

"You girls taking the train home after class?" she asked, not even looking them.

"No, our private helicopter is picking us up on top of the Pan Am building," Jennifer said very seriously as Polly stifled a giggle.

"Oh, you are *so* funny, dearheart. I only asked because my mother is stopping by on her way back from Bloomies and said she'd take you two. I told her you probably wouldn't be interested in a ride," she added as she tiptoed out of the dressing room.

"Do you think you could arrange for a house to fall on her, like it did on the Wicked Witch of the East?" Jennifer frowned, standing up on her toes.

"I'll try," Polly said, tying the ribbons of her toe shoe, "but I think a tribe of cannibals with poison darts would be more effective."

They heard the opening chords of the next class and hurried to take their places. Polly's feet ached, but she knew that after another hour of class, they would be numb and she wouldn't feel a thing. Polly was physically exhausted but also stimulated by the thought that class would end early today for announcements. She listened to the Chopin étude that accompanied her slow, graceful movements, and she tried to make it calm her inside and out. When that didn't work, she thought of a chocolate ice cream soda.

Ten minutes before the end of class, Mme Mishkin rapped her stick hard, and Joey gathered up his music while the girls took seats on the floor. Polly massaged her aching limbs, and Jennifer looking worried, curled her legs tightly under her. After Joey had walked out of the studio, Mme Mishkin cleared her throat and began to speak in clear, carefully enunciated English.

"Now, girlsss," she said, examining each anxious face in turn, "as you know, I haf received the names of the finalists from the Connecticut College scholarship program. Their decision was based, not only on your owditions last spring at the college but also on my recommendation from the work each of you has done since that time.

"Dance, particularly ballet"—she threw her arms into the air, as if praying to her own personal dance god—"is a grave responsibility. And you are aware, of course, that it will take work, painful years of work, if you intend to make ballet your life."

Polly shifted her weight restlessly and looked over at Jennifer, who was biting her thumbnail. *Make ballet your life*, she thought solemnly. It sounded so final. Of course she wanted to dance more than anything—but there were other things she had to do, too. Mme Mishkin went on and on about being totally and completely committed until Polly wanted to scream. *Why does she have to talk so much?* Polly agonized. She wiped drops of perspiration from her forehead, but they were more from nervousness than from the exertion of the last few hours.

"The competition does not end here," Mme Mishkin was saying. "There is only one scholarship to be given. And so, three of you here will haf to prove yourselves again and fight the necessary battle to win what you deserve. The last owdition is three weeks from Thursday in Town Hall."

Jennifer gave Polly a look. Above all, she didn't want to compete with her best friend. And Polly felt the same way.

"The names of the finalists are," Mme Mishkin proclaimed at last, "Dawn Sims"—Dawn jumped from her place on the floor and hugged herself, a look of enormous triumph on her face—"Jennifer Taruskin—"

"Oh, Jen!" Polly threw her arms around her friend. "I knew it!"

"And Polly Luria," Mme Mishkin finished.

Jennifer squealed with delight, and the two girls clutched each other as their classmates somewhat halfheartedly congratulated them and then, with looks of dejection on their faces, straggled back into the dressing room. Dawn, however, was smiling broadly.

"Oh, it's so wonderful!" Polly breathed. "I'm so happy for you."

14

"But *you're* going to get it," Jennifer insisted, pulling playfully at Polly's tightly rolled hair.

Polly clutched Jennifer's hands and pulled her to her feet. "As long as it's *one* of us," she said fiercely. "That's the only thing that matters!"

Chapter Two

Polly sat in Miss Burstein's advanced English class, only half-listening to the teacher's endless description of imagery in Shakespeare's *A Midsummer Night's Dream*. It was hard to concentrate on something as ordinary as language when what was really important was how great she and Jennifer would be as Helena and Hermia in the ballet. Poor, tall Helena chasing around the woods after Demetrius while short little Hermia, just as cranky as Jennifer, blamed her best friend for stealing her boyfriend Lysander. The parts were perfect for them.

Polly was so absorbed in thought that she almost didn't hear the bell ring for the end of class and was still half in a daydream when Jennifer yanked her out of her seat and began dragging her down the hallway to the staircase. Both girls were wearing long-sleeved, black, scooped-neck leotards under their jeans, in preparation for the long afternoon practice session they had scheduled in Sally Lipset's basement. Mrs. Lipset, a former dancer herself, had a fully equipped ballet studio right in her own home, and the girls were allowed to use it anytime they wanted.

"Hey, hold on!" exclaimed Polly as she dropped her knapsack and books spilled everywhere.

"I don't want you to miss him!" Jennifer insisted.

"I can see him tomorrow—I gotta go dance now."

"Come *on*." Jennifer pulled Polly down the stairs two at a time, despite her friend's vehement protests that this was no time to sprain an ankle with the final scholarship auditions only two weeks away. But Jennifer did not stop until they were at the door of Mamaroneck High's chemistry lab.

"Look—over there." She pointed through the glass panel in the top of the door toward the last long table in the back. At first Polly could only see Andy Donahue, who was pouring some vile-looking mixture from one beaker to another. Andy was considered Jennifer's boyfriend by everyone except Jennifer herself. He was still as crazy about her as he had been freshman year, and although she liked him as a friend, she was just not, as she confided to Polly, "sent reeling out of the stratosphere" when she spent time with him.

Then Polly saw the boy Jennifer was so excited about having her meet. He was really tall—even taller than Polly, which was something of a miracle—and very big in a muscular, well-built way. He had on a yellow Lacoste T-shirt, khaki pants, and an expensive-looking lizard-skin belt. His wavy brown hair, which was long in back, had deep red highlights. It was hard to tell what he really looked like because he had on dark glasses, but the overall effect was certainly impressive.

"Well, you want to meet him?" Jennifer was anxiously watching the class clean up. She pushed Polly away from the door so they wouldn't be caught spying. "Andy's bringing him to the Entertainment Committee meeting at—oh, my gosh!" she yelped, looking at her watch. "It's now!"

"You check him out for me." Polly smiled, slinging her knapsack over one shoulder. "What's his name again? Gott? Mott?"

"It's *Cott*. Cott Townsend."

"I never heard that name before."

"Me, either. Oh, hi, Andy." Jennifer smiled brightly to the boy who had just made his appearance in the doorway. He was short and slight, with thick straight dark hair, fantastic brown eyes, and a wonderful smile that grew even wider when he saw the girls.

"Hi, Jen. Hello, Polly. Say, we better get a move on—we're going to be late."

Jennifer turned to her friend and pointedly looked over Andy's shoulder to the person just walking out of the chem lab. "Why don't you walk with us, Pol?" She pronounced the words carefully, trying to make them match up with her eye movements.

"Huh-uh." Polly shook her head. "I've got to work on my audition piece. See you later at Sally's."

She began to walk down the corridor, but Jennifer ran to catch up with her, her face determined and slightly annoyed. "You go ahead, Andy," she called over her shoulder. "I'll catch up in a second. Start the meeting without me." She grabbed Polly's elbow and steered her into an empty classroom, then closed the door firmly behind them.

"*What* were we saying last weekend about us and boys?" she demanded.

Polly sighed and looked at the ceiling. "That we don't know enough of them."

"Right. And *who* doesn't have a date for the Harvest Ball?"

"Me, but—" Polly knew she was fighting a losing battle.

"Now here you have the perfect opportunity to meet a real live senior, Cott Townsend, transfer student from Beverly Hills High, who just happens to be the most gorgeous guy since Harrison Ford, only younger, and what do you do? You walk away. Honestly, I don't know what

I'm going to do with you," she finished, her hands on her hips.

Polly smiled at her best friend. "Just because I go to this meeting with you doesn't mean he's going to ask me out. And anyway, it's too pushy. That's not the way I want to meet a guy."

"Polly, they don't come on white horses and sweep you up anymore. Times have changed. You have to at least help them along."

Polly laughed. "If you think he's so terrific, why are you shoving him at me?"

"I didn't say I thought he was terrific. I haven't even met him yet. I just like the way he looks. Anyhow, there's Andy. . . ."

"Y-e-e-s?" Polly drew the word out and sat down on top of the nearest desk. She knew she was keeping Jennifer from her meeting, but they had agreed a long time ago that talks like this were important.

"Well, you know Andy. He's smart and nice and just oozes common sense."

"*And* he just happens to be the handsomest person in the junior class."

"That's true. But I wish he were taller."

"Don't be superficial. What else?" Polly fixed her friend with an intense stare.

"Oh, he never argues with anything I have to say—and I know I'm not right all the time."

"Jennifer, there is no one I know—or *you* know, for that matter—as kind as Andy. Who sat with you all last winter when you had that

21

lousy cold for weeks and your mom wouldn't let you go out? He could have signed on as a professional nurse!"

"Yes, you're right." Jennifer sighed. "I'm an ingrate. It's just that—well, I don't think he's my type." She stopped and looked at her shoes. "Except I don't know what my type is."

"Your type," Polly said, "is Mikhail Baryshnikov."

"Yeah, sure." Jennifer started for the door, but then she thought of something and turned back at her friend. "I mean, it's okay for now going out with Andy. But when you think about the rest of your life—and who you want to share it with—dating Andy takes on a new meaning. Anyone knows you can't share promises and secrets and stuff with a short guy who never argues."

"Jennifer!" Polly got up and gave her friend a gentle push. "Don't be so serious, for heaven's sake. You don't have to settle the future of the Western world right now, junior year. All you have to do is go out on dates. Just cool it."

"Polly," Jennifer said as they stepped back into the corridor together, "I can't give my body to someone who isn't the real item."

"You sure are something, you know that?" Polly laughed. "Have fun at your meeting and check this Cott person out thoroughly, okay? I expect full report when you get to Sally's. Bye!"

She skipped down the short flight of steps to the main floor.

"Bye." Jennifer waved after her. Suddenly she looked at her watch again and gasped. At a dead run, she made straight for the student lounge, where the Entertainment Committee had already been in session for fifteen minutes.

"Well, thank you for joining us," commented Steve Owen, the head of the committee. He glanced around at the six others in the room, and at last his gaze rested on Cott Townsend, who was sitting by himself at the end of the table.

"Cott, this is Jennifer. Jennifer, Cott."

"Hi," she nodded, trying to examine his face behind his aviator glasses. She thought he was good-looking, but she had never seen him without his dark glasses.

"Really sorry," Jennifer said. "I didn't realize—"

"Okay, sit down. We were just talking about decorating the gym. So why do we have to do this? I thought that was the Decorating Committee."

Andy had saved Jennifer a seat, and she slid into it as Mary Wanamaker explained the situation to Steve. "Sandy Peter's mother is in the hospital, so her head isn't really in this. I volunteered for us to take charge of everything."

"Okay," Steve said nodding. "Who's got ideas?"

"I'd like to do the place up sort of country and western," suggested Barbara Moffat, a pudgy girl with pigtails and large, horn-rimmed glasses. "We could get bales of hay and pitchforks and stuff."

"That's awful," Jennifer blurted out, and Andy pinched her to shut her up. "Ow! I mean, the band isn't a country band, so that'll just look silly." She shook her long blond hair over one shoulder and stole a glance at Cott Townsend, who was staring off into space.

"Well, if you don't like *my* idea," Barbara said pouting, "let's hear one of your own. Remember, we're not doing *Swan Lake*. This is a *dance* dance."

Jennifer shook her head and exchanged glances with Andy. "Well, Polly and I were talking the other day—"

"Yeah, what else is new," interrupted Stanley Price, who had once asked Polly out. "They're always talking."

"And we thought," Jennifer continued, "that it might be neat to do the gym like a nightclub. You know, good lighting and candles on little tables. Maybe some mirrors and potted palms," she went on expansively, getting carried away with her idea.

"Great, wonderful!" Steve enthused. "I like that, Jennifer. Only where do we get this terrific lighting and everything? That's gonna cost."

Andy leaned forward and put his elbows on the table, resting his head in his hands. "My dad's a florist," he said in his soft, mellow voice.

"If I can persuade him, maybe we could borrow some palms from him."

"That sounds good. Who else has an influential father?" Steve joked.

"I do." It was Cott Townsend. "I could get some lights and mirror panels, easy," he nodded, pulling off his dark glasses.

Jennifer looked at him closely. His eyes were gray and deep-set, and he had prominent cheekbones, a full mouth, and a slightly crooked nose that looked as if he'd broken it a long time ago. Jennifer was impressed by the fact that even though none of his features was particularly stunning in and of itself, the way they all went together was fantastic.

"What's your dad do, Cott?" simpered Barbara Moffat.

"He's a TV producer," Cott said simply, in a low, musical voice. "He does a lot of specials here and on the Coast."

"Not Mitchell Townsend!" Jennifer squealed suddenly. "*The* Mitchell Townsend?"

"Who's Mitchell Townsend?" Barbara muttered under her breath.

"Uh-huh." Cott smiled smugly. "He's why I'm here, see. He just moved his field of operations to New York."

A ripple of admiration traveled around the table. Interest in the Harvest Ball had just shifted to curiosity about Cott's father.

"Hey, well, that's great, really great." Steve

nodded. "We could use some strobe lights and maybe a mirrored ball—you know, the ones that turn and catch the light, and—"

"Back home," Cott interrupted, "we don't need all that stuff to have a party, man. I mean, we just get high and boogie."

Jennifer's estimation of Cott fell at once. What kind of comment was that, anyway? She flashed him a disgusted look, but he was staring into space again, not really paying attention. All she could think of was how totally California he seemed and how she disliked that. "Well, back East," she barked, "we do things differently."

His laid-back expression changed, and just for a second, he looked embarrassed. "Ah, sure, Jennifer. 'When in Rome,' right? So, if you guys want the lights, I'll get 'em. No sweat."

"Terrific, Cott. Okay, is everyone agreed on this nightclub idea?" Steve asked, looking around.

There were assorted murmurs of "yeah" and "okay" from the committee members.

"Good. It's set, then. Cott's in charge of lighting, Andy gets the plants. Barbara and Mary, can you manage the candles and tables? Stan, why don't you figure how to rig those mirrors? And Jennifer—well, you're the artistic one. Why don't you be music coordinator and make sure the band is up on—well, whatever kind of music you have in nightclubs."

"Okay," Jennifer agreed.

"Meeting adjourned," Steve announced as the group began straggling away from the table. Jennifer noticed that Cott was out the door before anyone else.

"How about a Coke?" Andy asked as Jennifer picked up her book bag.

"Can't. There're only a couple more weeks till the audition, and I have to meet Polly to practice. The nerve of that guy," she added, stamping her foot for emphasis. She walked quickly ahead of Andy into the corridor.

"Who?"

"Cott. The way he throws around that California stuff. 'Get high and boogie'! I mean, really!"

"I don't know—he seems like a nice guy." Andy shook his head. "Don't get all worked up. You sure you don't want a Coke?" He was still smiling, but it was clear he knew he wasn't about to change her mind.

"Sure. Walk me to the bike rack. I can't stand laid-back people." She marched down the last steps and out the front door of the school.

"I'll call you tonight after dinner," Andy told her, helping her slip her book bag under the rack on her bike and secure it with elastic cord.

"Okay. And Andy"—she stopped with her leg in the air, about to ride off—"if you get my mother on the phone, could you *please* not tell her absolutely everything I've ever told you? Please?"

"Sure, Jennifer." Andy laughed. "I will attempt to keep my mouth shut—just for you. Have a good practice."

"Thanks, bye." She pedaled off, her hair a golden banner flying behind her. But on her way to Sally Lipset's house, she wasn't thinking about Andy. She was thinking about Cott.

"I take it all back. You wouldn't like him," she insisted, sliding onto the floor in a split. She took the towel that Polly offered her and slung it around her neck.

"Jennifer, he said *one* thing you didn't happen to like, and suddenly he's public enemy number one. Sounds sort of interesting to me. Sounds like he's independent, not a groupie. I like that." She collapsed in a heap beside her friend. They had been working for three hours straight in Sally Lipset's basement on their individual dance combinations for the audition, and they were exhausted.

"It's not just what he said, Polly. It's his attitude. You know those sophisticated, obnoxious kids who think they're cool because they smoke and drink and do drugs."

Polly sat up and put her hands on top of her head. "Oh, spare me! Spare me! The evils of the world!" she moaned in mock distress.

"What's with you?" Jennifer looked very flustered.

"Look." Polly got serious again. "I've told you

for years that you're much too judgmental. You don't know for a fact that this guy is punk-decadent—you're just guessing it from one thing he said. Boy, I'm glad you didn't decide I was a stuck-up ballet snob the first time you met me."

"That's different." Jennifer got up and went to the barre to escape Polly's close scrutiny. A couple of drops of perspiration fell from her dripping hair onto the wood floor.

"It isn't. Now, start from the beginning and tell me something good about this Cott." Polly wrapped her arms around her knees and waited.

"I don't know why you say these things. I'm no more judgmental than you are."

"Oh, great. I have some pretty strong opinions, too, sometimes. Not something I'm always proud of. Didn't we decide that was why Stanley Price never asked me out again? I told him how I thought people who went bowling were dumb as he drove us into the parking lot of the bowling alley."

"Real tact." Jennifer giggled. "Okay, well, maybe you have a point."

"So"—Polly walked over to her tote bag and began fishing around inside it—"tell me about Cott."

"Well, he's gorgeous."

"I know that. What else?"

"I don't think he has a girlfriend. Andy said he generally hangs around after school to use the swimming pool, and Cott once offered him a lift home. He's got this really great MG."

"Pretty neat." Polly was now definitely sure she wanted to meet Cott Townsend. "What do his parents do, you know?"

"Well, his father is a real big-shot TV producer. He must eat caviar for breakfast. Remember that Gene Kelly special last spring? The night you stayed over at my house."

"Oh, sure. His father did that?"

"Uh-huh. Cott didn't make a big thing about his dad, but he did offer to get us lights and mirrors for the Harvest Ball free of charge."

"See, there's something positive! I knew he had to have one redeeming quality."

"Polly!" Jennifer threw the towel into her tote bag and eased out of her toe shoes. "You're *very* funny. When is your mom coming by?"

"Right about now. Wait a sec—I want to show you something. Here it is." She pulled a copy of *Glamour* from her knapsack and quickly flipped pages until she came to a particular photo. "How do you like this?" She spread the magazine on the floor in front of them.

It was part of a clothing layout. The picture in question was of a tall, gangly redhead wearing a flowered French-schoolgirl smock dress. Her hair was clipped neatly in a pretty style— short yet feminine, with romantic wisps and tendrils around her face.

"Nice dress." Jennifer threw a sweater around

her shoulders, then put the rest of her gear inside her tote.

"I mean the hair."

"Uh, it's okay, I guess. Why?"

"Well, I'm getting my hair cut tomorrow, and I've decided to have it done this way."

Jennifer's face registered shock. "You're kidding, right? That's a joke."

"No, I'm tired of wearing it long." She pulled her thick dark braid apart and began drying the damp strands with her towel.

"Polly," Jennifer said sternly, "you've had some dumb ideas in the past, but this one is the dumbest. You can't cut your hair! Especially not before the competition."

"Why not?" Polly smiled. "It'll be much easier to take care of."

"Dancers have long hair, period."

"Who says?"

"Come on, Pol. Name me one ballerina without lots of hair."

"There're plenty of them."

"*Name* one."

Polly stood there, staring at her friend, unwilling to admit defeat. "I can't think of one offhand," she said evenly. "But I know there are some."

"To make it in this business," Jennifer persisted, "you have to have long hair."

"And small breasts, I know. Jennifer, what is with you these days?" Polly asked, genuinely concerned. "First you tell me I can't go out with a boy who makes one comment you don't like. Then you tell me I can't cut my hair."

Jennifer stalked away, over to the basement stairs. She refused to say anything, but Polly could tell she was very hurt.

"Jennifer," she said softly, following her to the stairs, "I'm not trying to be mean. I just want you to hear what you're saying."

"Oh, go ahead and do whatever you want," Jennifer stormed at her. "It's only because you're my best friend that I tell you these things, but I guess you don't care about that anymore." She yanked the door open and marched into the Lipset kitchen.

Polly bit her lip and choked back an angry response. She felt hot tears welling up behind her eyes. What was going on between them? Was it because they were competing against one another for the scholarship? *If it means losing Jennifer's friendship,* she told herself miserably, *I don't want to win.* But then, as she closed the basement door behind her, she admitted the truth: she *did* want to win—she wanted to very badly.

Her mother was already waiting for them in Sally's kitchen, so there was no opportunity to either continue the argument or smooth things over.

"Hi, Mom." Polly went over and kissed her on the cheek, conscious of her mother's curious expression. Jane Luria always knew when something was up with Polly.

"Hi, girls. You two work hard today?" Mrs. Luria's warm brown eyes shifted to Jennifer's face.

"Yeah, we really did," Jennifer said, not looking at Mrs. Luria.

Polly turned to Mrs. Lipset, a tall, skinny blond in her early fifties. "Thanks, Sally. Bye."

Jennifer tried to smile, but she was holding back a flood of tears. Solemnly the two girls walked their bikes to the Luria car and lifted them onto the bike rack.

"I spoke to that guy in New York for you today, Polly," Mrs. Luria mentioned as she unlocked the door of their Toyota and moved several bags of groceries so that the girls could climb in.

"Who's that, Mom?"

"The hairdresser, ah, Philippe, isn't that his name? You're all set for tomorrow at four-thirty."

"Okay," Polly murmured glumly. Jennifer wouldn't look at her.

As Mrs. Luria started the car and drove off down Sylvan Avenue, the two girls stared out the windows on either side of the car. Neither of them could think of a thing to say.

Chapter Three

"Hurry up, Nancy, would you *please!*" Jennifer pounded at the bathroom door while Polly leaned back against the opposite wall. "You've been in there forever, and we have to get ready for the dance."

There was no response other than the sound of water running in the sink.

"Oh, Pol!" Jennifer exclaimed, but just at that moment, the door opened, and Nancy Taruskin slowly walked out. She was taller than her sister, had a pale, pretty face, and wore rimless glasses. Her hair was shoulder length, and she pulled it straight back with a headband so that it wouldn't get in her eyes when she was working some particularly difficult mathematical computation. Nancy was a year ahead of her sister at Mamaroneck High, and according to Jennifer, she was on the road to becoming the Isaac Newton of the twentieth century. But because she never dated or went to school functions, it was hard for her to understand the urgency about a mere dance.

"Hi, Nancy." Polly grinned, wedging the bathroom door open with one foot, just in case Nancy got any ideas about going back inside.

"Ah—hello." Her clear blue eyes fixed on Polly, but it took her a second to make the conection. No matter that Polly was over at the Taruskin home all the time; Nancy's head was elsewhere.

Jennifer barged past her older sister, giving her a look, and Polly followed her inside, flipping down the cover on the toilet seat so she could sit on it.

"What's the look for tonight?" Polly asked.

"Um, let's see." Jennifer retrieved her makeup case from under the sink and began lining up a variety of shadow sticks and rouges. The girls never wore makeup to school—only for performances and social functions, like tonight's Harvest Ball.

"I'll have some Smoke Haze on my lids, and just a touch of gleamer under the brows and on the cheekbones. Then mascara and blusher and I'm set. How about you?" she handed the kit to Polly, who immediately began outlining the inside of Jennifer's lower lids with a dark blue pencil. They always did each other's makeup.

"How would I look in serious punk?" she teased, smearing blue-gray on Jennifer's lids.

"Hey, you want to *talk* to Cott Townsend, not scare him to death."

"Okay then, no makeup."

"How dull. Look, let me decide." She swung around to examine herself in the mirror, and, having approved of the additions to her naturally peachy complexion, she drew Polly alongside her.

"I know, let me do exactly what I did for the competition on Thursday." As soon as the words were out of her mouth, she was sorry. After the competition was over, the girls had vowed not to mention it again, not to think about it until the letters arrived from Connecticut College telling them whether or not they had made it.

"Hmm," Polly said, looking into Jennifer's eyes in the mirror, "don't you think that dance makeup is a little extreme?"

"You may be right," Jennifer said. "I'll just do you all smudged—okay?"

"Sure." The girls were very subdued as Jennifer went to work. Neither of them had ever alluded to their argument about Polly's haircut. In fact, as soon as Polly had returned from the City with her new short cut, she had gone right over to Jennifer's to show her. The hairdresser had tied her long, shorn locks together with a rubber band and folded them neatly in a paper bag, in case she ever wanted to have them made into a hairpiece to wear for performances. Jennifer had scrutinized her friend's new look and,

after a long moment, had pronounced it spec-
tacular. Polly's brown eyes seemed even bigger,
and the effect of the tendrils escaping from all
sides was completely feminine. But although
Jennifer was enthusiastic in her careful, guarded
way, it was clear to both girls that something
had happened to the friendship. It was not something either one of them could point to as a real
change; instead, it was a difference in attitude.
When Polly thought about it all, it made her
very sad. But as her mother had often told her,
even before she divorced Polly's father, "there
is no such thing as complete togetherness."

Polly watched Jennifer smooth some blusher
across her cheek, and she made herself a promise. If Jennifer won the scholarship, she would
not let that make the friendship disintegrate
faster. But she wondered—and worried—if *she*
won, what would Jennifer do?

Well, she thought, as Jennifer handed her
her mother's bottle of Fidji for a quick dab
behind each ear, there was nothing she could
do about it now. The actual decision had been
made on Thursday in Town Hall. Even though
she had vowed she wouldn't think about it,
Polly couldn't stop herself from reviewing the
final audition one more time.

They had been given two days off at school,
and Mrs. Luria took them into the City both
days. Mme Mishkin had been in a real state on

38

Wednesday, screaming at Dawn for messing up a couple of difficult combinations and admonishing Polly for not working hard enough. At the end of a very long day, she had sent them home to rest, reminding them of their "grave responsibility."

"I am not caring which of you three wins," she had said. "But one of you must."

Thursday morning at Town Hall was mass confusion. There was a small dressing room area where the girls had put on their makeup and done their hair. Oddly enough, Mme Mishkin hadn't even mentioned Polly's haircut—there was just too much else to think about.

Jennifer, Polly, Dawn, and the seven other girls had taken their places onstage while an assistant ran around adjusting the number tags they wore on their leotards. Then the music for the barre began, and an instructor gave them a rudimentary warmup. After that came the really hard part. When Jennifer and Polly compared notes later in the car, they decided that the worst things were the blinding stagelights that kept them from seeing anyone in the audience. They had no idea whether the judges were pleased or disgusted. And they both agreed that while they were furiously concentrating on positions and the height of their leaps, they couldn't help but compare themselves to the other girls onstage. Polly picked one candidate, a really gorgeous Oriental girl from Rhode Island, whom she was certain was the winner. But Jennifer disagreed.

The final test of the day, after they had all been working for three hours with only one fifteen-minute break, was that each dancer had to do a solo. Jennifer did a classical piece from *Coppélia* that was perfectly suited to her neat little form, and Polly did a dramatic section of *Giselle*. "Even with that weird haircut," Jennifer announced grudgingly when Polly exited in the wings, "there's no one who could do that better. You were fantastic."

In a week they would have the results. Until then, they just had to go on living like normal teenagers, impossible as that seemed.

"Would you stand still?" Polly fastened the top hooks on Jennifer's sky-blue handkerchief linen dress. It had an uneven hem and leg-of-mutton sleeves and seemed to dance by itself. As Mme Mishkin would have said, it "moved well." With her hair wound in an elaborate series of braids, Jennifer looked like a modern fairy-tale princess.

Polly, in contrast, was wearing a dress of her mother's from the fifties. It was a chocolate brown rayon sheath with a mesh insert at the top of the bodice, and it fit Polly's long figure as though it had been sewn right on her. Two long panels at the waist were drawn back into a drape that swayed whenever she moved.

The two girls descended the staircase slowly, arm in arm, and presented themselves solemnly to Dr. and Mrs. Taruskin, who were waiting for them in the den before starting dinner. Nancy was sitting in an armchair, doodling on a piece of graph paper.

"My God!" Dr. Taruskin dropped his newspaper and gawked at the girls. "Strangers have broken into our house. Who are you two?"

"You both look lovely," Mrs. Taruskin said distractedly, starting for the kitchen. "I only hope you don't get dinner all over your dresses."

"It's okay, Mom." Jennifer followed her into the next room. "We really don't want anything to eat."

Her mother faced her and gave her a stern glance. "Jennifer, I don't want to hear any of this anorexia nonsense."

"What?" Jennifer laughed.

"Are you kidding? With *my* appetite?" Polly added. "She just meant we'd eat stuff at the dance, Mrs. Taruskin."

"Chips and pretzels!" Jennifer's mother snorted as the two girls exchanged looks. "I know all about young dancers starving themselves. It's a terrible disease, anorexia, and impossible to cure."

Jennifer's father came up behind her and put his hands on her shoulders. "Who's the doctor around here?" he asked gruffly. "Don't pick at them, Joanne. Their appetites are just fine. And they will continue to be so unless you turn them into nervous nellies. Okay, girls, I'll drive you over to the dance now, if you like." He bent over to kiss his wife and whispered something in her ear that made her smile.

"Can we go, Mom?" Jennifer asked anxiously.

"Well, I suppose." Mrs. Taruskin opened the refrigerator door and pulled some carrot sticks out of the vegetable bin. "Will you at least take these for the ride?"

Jennifer grabbed them and stuck one in her mouth. "Thanks a lot. We'll be home early, promise. Andy's dad said he'd pick us up at eleven or so." The girls hurried to the front coat closet for their jackets.

"Have a lovely time, dears," called Joanne Taruskin as the door closed behind them.

The night was very cool, and there was a huge moon hanging in the sky. In the glare of the street lamps, Polly could see the maples on the block in all their glory, every one crimson and gold. She just had a feeling that something wonderful was about to happen.

Tonight, maybe, she'd succeed in forgetting about the audition. Tonight she wanted to have a good time and not go over and over the mistakes she'd made. Maybe tonight at the dance she'd be able to put everything out of her mind and imagine how life would be without Mme Mishkin and injured toes and continual practice. Maybe tonight, like Cinderella at the ball, she'd feel a part of things and less like an outsider. But then she glanced over at Jennifer's intense face and decided that it would never work. There was just too much going on in her life right now to start wanting to be like everybody else.

The minute she entered the gym, though, she knew it was going to be a great night, no matter what happened.

"How d'ya like it?" Jennifer asked proudly, throwing her jacket onto the mounting pile of coats and dragging Polly around to get a look at the decor.

"It's—well, positively incredible. Like a stage set! How did you ever do this?" After coming home exhausted from the audition Thursday night, Jennifer had hauled herself back to school and the task of decorating. Then after classes were over on Friday, the committee had spent five more hours on the refinements. Now Mamaroneck High's gymnasium could almost have passed for a large supper club in Manhattan, if you forgot about the basketball hoops. The walls had been lined with mirrors, and potted palms stood like soldiers at attention at odd intervals. The lighting was dramatic but unobtrusive, and a large mirrored ball turned in slow circles above a silver-draped bandstand. Small tables decorated with snowy white tablecloths and candles in glass globes dotted the room.

"It's so romantic," Polly breathed. "Now if I

only had something to feel romantic about," she quipped. Ben Almeida, the bandleader, waved at her, and she smiled and waved back. He began getting the attention of his band members, since it was time to start the music.

"Hey, there he is! Look." Jennifer wheeled Polly around so that she was facing the front door of the gym. "*What* is he wearing? He looks fantastic!"

Cott Townsend didn't look like any of the other juniors or seniors now straggling into the Harvest Ball. Word had been sent around that no one was to come in jeans, no matter what, and that jackets were requested, although not actually demanded, of the guys. But Cott definitely stood out in the crowd. He was casually but dashingly dressed in a modified Civil War uniform—navy blue twill with two rows of silver buttons narrowing from his shoulders to his waist. He was standing by himself at the door, a small smile on his face, his dark glasses still masking his eyes.

"You know what I like about him?" Polly murmured, pulling at one of the wispy tendrils near her left ear. "He's so—unconcerned. I mean, he doesn't try to make an impression—he just does."

"Well, come on, I'll introduce you. I promised not to inflict any more of my opinions about him on you." Jennifer grinned, taking Polly by the hand.

They were halfway across the floor when Ben gave the downbeat and the band began to play.

But before they could reach Cott, Ellen Drake, the prettiest girl in the senior class, swooped down from nowhere and grabbed his arm. The girls watched her long, shiny hair bouncing up and down as she began flirting outrageously.

"Oh, well," Jennifer said, smiling encouragingly, "the night is young. And *you* are a vision of loveliness. Let's get a Coke."

The refreshments table was set up across the dance floor, and it was already crowded with students who only came to dances to stuff their faces and the chaperons who wanted to get as far from the loud rock music as possible. The band was now playing a wild rendition of "You Better, You Better, You Bet," and Polly could feel the floor vibrating beneath her. She wandered toward the cookie tray and took a couple of Oreos for sustenance.

"Hey, I've been looking for you," Andy Donahue exclaimed. He looked very preppy with his navy blazer, white pants, and a blue-and-white rep tie knotted tightly around his neck. He was smiling broadly, tapping his foot in time to the beat, and his thick, dark hair was struggling to get free of its temporary bondage—he'd wet it down at home to comb it into place, but it clearly had no intention of behaving. "Jennifer, wow, great sound, huh?" He nodded approvingly. "I mean, that man *makes music*." He punctuated the words as he spoke.

"Pretty good," she agreed, taking the hand he offered and allowing him to whirl her underneath his arm. Polly slipped out of the way to make room.

"Hey, that's neat." Jennifer smiled when he changed direction and didn't miss a beat. "You didn't used to be able to do that."

"Practice, practice." He grinned. Out of the side of his mouth, he told Polly, "I do it in front of the bathroom mirror at home in my spare time. Let me tell you, it's hard to steer clear of the towel rack."

Jennifer giggled and drew Andy out toward the center of the floor, where other couples were dancing. "See you, Pol," she called over her shoulder.

Interesting, Polly mused, watching them. *She actually looks like she's enjoying herself.*

She shuffled her feet in an approximation of a time-step. *That's the problem with school dances,* she mused, *the right people never know how to dance.* She stared at her reflection in one of the angled mirrors and told herself that even if she was a wallflower, she didn't look too awful tonight. *Maybe I'll be brave,* she thought, *and cut in on Ellen Drake. How else am I going to get to meet that guy?*

As she stood there, trying to get up her nerve, she felt a hand on her elbow. In the mirror she saw a tall blue form behind her and silver buttons glinting off the overhead lights.

"May I have this dance?" Cott Townsend made a gallant bow, and she turned, smiling, and stepped into his arms. "Hi," she said.

The music had switched, and the soft, gentle melody of "Penny Lane" gave them the opportunity for a slow dance. Cott held Polly lightly, not too close, and she was conscious of the fact that she had to reach up to rest her left hand on his shoulder. For a few seconds they swayed quietly together, and then he looked down at her and said, "I'm Cott Townsend."

"Polly Luria," she responded. "Ah—if it's not too personal a question, what kind of name is Cott?"

"Cott. For apricot."

"Oh." Polly didn't know whether or not to smile. "Well, of course that explains everything."

He shrugged. "When I was born, my two-year-old sister was really into dried apricots. It was the only thing she'd eat. And she called everything she saw apricot, including me. My real name's John."

"I think I like Cott better."

"Yeah, me, too. I mean, people always know who you are when you call them on the phone. Say"—he looked around the gym—"this is wild, man. I never went to one of these before."

"You've never been to a school dance?" Polly

47

raised her eyebrow skeptically. "You're putting me on."

"Hey, no, really. It's just at Beverly Hills High, you know, nobody's into formals. We just go down to the beach and hang out and turn on and ride the waves."

Polly took a breath and looked at him closely. He seemed awfully clean-cut, almost naive, for someone who claimed to be so hip.

"What do you turn on with?" she challenged him.

"Huh? Well, you know, grass and stuff."

"Oh?" she smiled slightly, obviously unimpressed.

"Well, that's what the scene is in L.A.," he insisted. "So you go with the flow."

"Aw, don't give me that." Polly laughed, as the band struck up "Looking for Love" and Cott attempted a clumsy two-step. "I bet you're the kind of guy who's into, um, I don't know, ecology, maybe. Not drugs."

"Oh, yeah?" he held her at arm's length and tried to figure out how much he could get away with.

"Yeah."

Then he burst out laughing. "Ecology? You are something else!" he exclaimed. "So tell me, what do you do when you're not looking glamorous at a school dance?" His intense gray eyes had an amused expression.

"I dance," she said casually.

"What do you mean?"

"Dancing, like, oh, you know." She whirled away from him and spun around twice on her toes.

"Wow, like ballet?" He grinned.

"Uh-huh."

"Hey, that's great. My mom used to dance. Well, stepmom, actually. She was pretty good."

"Really?" Polly's eyes were wide. "Which company was she with?"

"The Fandango Follies. Las Vegas chorus girls. With the feathers and sequins." Abruptly, he stopped dancing and led her off the floor, toward the door. As they stood, enjoying the cool air, Cott took off his glases, wiped them on his jacket, then put them back on.

"I can't see what you're thinking with those on," Polly grumbled. "Why do you wear them?"

"I'm nearsighted. Why else?" he admitted, shrugging. Polly began giggling uncontrollably. "What's so funny?"

"I don't know. I just feel good," she said, smiling.

"Me, too. Let's split, get some air or something. My MG's right outside."

She pursed her lips and tilted her head up toward him. "I really don't like it when you come on so strong, okay?" she said quietly.

He shrugged. "So we'll stay here. That's cool. How about another dance?"

"In a second. I'm going in there. Be right

back." She pointed toward the ladies' room, and he nodded.

"I'm not going anyplace," he said.

As Polly walked sedately across the gym, she felt a little ping of exhilaration start off like a bubble bursting in her head. Then it traveled down her arms to her fingertips and raced around her stomach before taking a mad dash to her feet. There was something about this guy, she decided, something deeper than his boastful, pseudosophisticated veneer. He was putting on an act, and she was determined to see right through it.

Jennifer was standing with Andy watching the dancers on the floor, and when Polly indicated where she was going, Jennifer followed her.

"Well, I *saw* you." Jennifer was almost jumping up and down with excitement. "What's he like?"

"A good dancer with a nice personality," Polly said teasingly.

"*Polly!* This is me, remember? Is he like I said?"

Polly got serious for a second as she reached into her tiny evening bag for a comb. "Well, partly. But he's different, too."

"How different? Why aren't you talking to me?" Jennifer pouted. "He was *my* idea, you know."

Polly turned on her friend. "Well, thanks for the idea. And I can take it from here!" Jennifer's mouth dropped open in shock and hurt.

Polly sighed and took her friend's hand. "Oh, I'm sorry. I don't know why we're always fighting lately. Just a lot to think about, I guess."

Jennifer nodded, but her expression did not soften.

"What I meant was, I'm trying not to judge him on a first impression—yours *or* mine. I'll let you know if anything's going to happen."

"I would hope so." The words were barely audible.

"Jennifer, of course I will! What do you think? Come on, let's get back." Together they walked out of the bathroom, and after Polly had left her friend with an anxiously waiting Andy Donahue, she started back to the corner where she'd left Cott.

But he wasn't there. Sighing slightly, she turned and swayed to the band's somewhat jerky version of "Just the Way You Are." Then she saw him. He was smiling at her, holding out two paper cups of Coke.

"Thought I lost you," he admonished her as he walked over and handed her a glass.

She shook her head. "Did I miss any good numbers?"

"Nope. This is one of my favorites. Shall we?" They downed their drinks, set the glasses down on a table, then moved into each other's arms. This time Cott held her firmly, but not too tight, and she closed her eyes letting him lead.

"You wanna know a secret?" he asked her at last.

Her eyes flew open. "Ah, yeah, I guess so."

"Promise you won't tell."

"Promise."

"I don't do any drugs. I just like to talk big sometimes." He smiled weakly.

"Uh-huh."

"That all you're gonna say?"

"Yup. Now shut up and dance."

On Monday he asked her for a date. She was on her way out the front door of school when she felt a hand on her arm.

"Excuse me," a deep male voice said. "Uh—hi, how are you?"

"Oh, great! I mean, pretty good." Polly stammered. She just couldn't take her eyes off him. He was wearing beautifully cut brown corduroy slacks and a brown-and-blue weave wool shirt open at the collar.

"So—" Cott said, smiling, "you busy or anything?"

"You mean now?"

"Sure. No time like immediately." He grinned. "As the minutes flash by, we could be getting to know each other, right?"

"Well, I—" She was supposed to be at dance practice. But hadn't Jennifer agreed that she didn't know enough guys? And she never sluffed off, *ever*. Just this once wouldn't hurt. "I'd love to."

"Terrific. How about Joe's? It's in walking distance."

"Okay." Together they continued down the front steps, and Polly's arm accidentally brushed his. She jerked aside quickly, and he laughed.

"First date, boy. It's tough."

"How do you mean?" She looked at him curiously, surprised that he'd even mention it. Boys just didn't talk about things like that.

"Well, you know. If this were our second date, I could, like, hold your hand. If it were our third date, maybe I'd put my arm around you. But on the first date, you're wary. We're like two lions circling each other, sizing each other up." He danced around her, baring imaginary fangs, and she giggled.

"I see what you mean."

They had reached Joe's, a popular hangout where a lot of kids came after school. But the place was quiet this afternoon, and Polly and Cott found a choice booth near the back. They slid in on opposite sides and stared at one another. There was an awkward silence.

"Did you have a nice weekend?" they both suddenly blurted out at the same moment.

Cott shook his head and pointed a finger at her forehead. "Two minds with but a single thought."

She was about to answer when the waitress

slapped two menus on the table. "Gonna order now or should I come back?" she asked.

"Just black coffee for me," Polly stated, pushing her menu aside.

"No way," Cott frowned. He leaned over toward her conspiratorially. "Look, this is our first date and I want it to be special. What would you order if you weren't thinking about dancing and watching your weight?"

"Well, I always have coffee," Polly admitted. "But if I were really splurging, I guess I'd have an eggcream."

"Eggcream? What's eggcream? It sounds awful."

Polly laughed. "Don't tell me you've never heard of an eggcream?"

"Nope," Cott said, "I never have. What is it?"

"It's a drink," Polly explained, "and I don't know why it's called that because there are no eggs or cream in it. It's made of milk, chocolate syrup, and seltzer. You fill a glass about one-third of the way with cold milk, add chocolate syrup, stir it, then fill the glass to the top with seltzer or carbonated water, and stir it again. That's it. It's delicious."

"Make it two," Cott said to the waitress, who was impatiently shifting her weight from one foot to the other. She wrote down the order, then walked away.

Polly smiled broadly at Cott. She was having an incredibly good time, and she hadn't thought about ballet or Jennifer in nearly half an hour. "I shouldn't have chocolate," she confided. "But, well, you only live once, right?"

"You said it." Cott's hands were lying on the table so close to hers that she almost pulled back, but then she decided it was time to relax and enjoy this date.

"Well, tell me," she asked, looking into his gray eyes, "what do you do after school in L.A.?"

"Oh, you know, the beach. That's the center of everything. If I were within driving distance of Venice right this second . . ." His eyes clouded over, and Polly wondered if he was homesick. "Boy," he said, taking a deep breath, "I'd give anything to be there now. The salt air, the smog, the freeways, it's—what can I say? It's what I'm used to, you know?"

"Hmm." Polly suddenly felt uneasy. Why was he telling her he'd rather be somewhere else? She couldn't really get excited about somebody who wanted to live in the past. "Well, it doesn't sound so great to me," she challenged.

"I think you'd like it if the right person showed it to you." He looked solemnly at her with his intense gray eyes.

"Maybe," she ventured, not at all sure.

"I promise you would. But I'll tell you something L.A. *doesn't* have that Mamaroneck does."

"Oh, what's that?" Polly tried not to sound too interested.

"You," he whispered. "And I guess that could make up for everything else."

Polly blushed. Maybe Cott Townsend was the only boy she needed to meet after all.

Chapter Four

The letters arrived two weeks later, a rainy Saturday morning in early November. Polly had been frantic for days, haranguing the postman and suggesting that maybe he had dropped the letters or lost them or something. But when the envelope finally came, embossed with the Connecticut College address in gold, Polly suddenly calmed down. As she held the letter between her fingers, she felt a great sense of relief wash over her. Her mother had gone out shopping; she was alone in the house with her thoughts, holding a letter that might spell her fate for the next two summers—maybe the next five years. Polly placed it on the hall table where she could stare at it and picked up the phone to dial Jennifer.

"Did you get it?" she asked anxiously.

"Yes." Jennifer's voice sounded hollow.

"I'll be right over."

They had made a pact to open them together. Polly threw a heavy poncho over her blue Western shirt and jeans, then pulled up the hood of the poncho to protect her hair from the cold drizzle. As she wheeled her bike out of the garage, she wondered whether this would be the end of the friendship. Her intuition told her that one of them was the winner, but it wasn't acute enough to determine which one.

"I guess Madame will be pretty ticked off," Jennifer said as she met her best friend at the door. "We're going to get to the city late."

"Everyone'll be late. Even Dawn. Everyone knew the letters were coming today." Polly took off her poncho and plopped herself down at the kitchen table, removing the letter from her pocket and placing it on the table in front of her. Mrs. Taruskin was baking her mother a birthday cake, and she scarcely noticed the somber mood of the two girls. Nancy was totally immersed in her Rubik's Cube.

"Well, let's go to my room," Jennifer suggested, slightly annoyed at the flurry of activity in the kitchen.

"No, I'd rather do it here." Polly felt that the comfort of having other people around might forestall a flood of tears.

"Oh, okay. You ready?" The girls ripped their letters down the side, and each withdrew one sheet of Connecticut College stationery from their envelopes. Together they unfolded the pieces of paper that would decide their fates.

Mrs. Taruskin stopped folding in her egg whites for a moment. "Don't keep me in suspense, girls. What's the verdict?" She looked from one face to the other, trying to get a hint.

"Oh, my God!" screamed Polly, jumping from her chair. She grabbed Jennifer and whirled her around the room.

"Oh, Polly! Congratulations!" Jennifer was laughing and crying at the same time.

"You, too! Oh, I'm so happy!" Polly spun away from her friend and ran over to embrace Joanne Taruskin, who looked completely confused and astonished. Both girls were now bounding back toward one another, laughing gleefully.

"Girls, what is—?" Mrs. Taruskin began.

"We won! We *both* won," Polly yelled in a delirium of joy, retrieving her letter from the table to show to her friend's mother.

"Mom, it's the very first time they ever gave two scholarships." Jennifer was practically hysterical.

Nancy looked up from her puzzle for a brief moment. "I'm really happy for you, Jen," she muttered. "You too, Polly." Then she went back to twisting the cube.

"What do we do first?" Polly's eyes shone with buoyant excitement. This had to be the greatest event in her life, ever—except for meeting

Cott, of course. As soon as she thought of him she wanted to call him.

"We have to phone Madame," Jennifer gasped. "And then we've got to catch our train. Oh, no!" she wailed, looking at her watch. "We can't make the nine-fifty."

Polly was already at the kitchen phone, dialing her house. She bounced from one foot to the other as the number rang three, four, five times. "Oh, she's not back yet. She said she was only going grocery shopping. Okay, what's Madame's phone number? Oh, I can't think straight!"

Mrs. Taruskin laughed and put down her baking utensils.

"Polly, you can leave your bike here. I'll drive both of you over to your house and you can pick up your things. Then I'll drive you to the station—you can make the next train if we hurry. Then I'll call Madame Mishkin and try to get your mother at the house later." She ticked off everything she had to do on her fingers.

"Well, what are we standing around for?" Jennifer grabbed her tote and threw on her raincoat. "Mom, can Pol and I do something to celebrate?"

"You know what I really want?" Polly sighed dizzily before Mrs. Taruskin could answer. "I'd just die if we could get seats to a Misha performance." She clapped her hands giddily at the thought of seeing Baryshnikov dance and unfolded Jennifer's letter to read it once again. "I've got about fifteen dollars at home. Do you think that'll do it?"

"Mom, can we go?" Jennifer hadn't stopped moving in the past ten minutes.

"Will you two let me get one word in?" Joanne Taruskin shook her head as she shrugged on her raincoat. "Now go get in the car, and, Jennifer, here's some money." She fumbled in her purse and pulled out two ten-dollar bills. "Don't tell your father and make sure you get tickets to one of the matinees. And you go *after* dance class to get them, not before. Can you remember all this? In your present state I'm not at all sure."

In a clamor of excitement, the girls managed to dash out through the now-steady downpour and get themselves into the car. Neither girl could shut up for a minute, and Polly felt tears of awe and wonder about to surface from under her totally blithering silliness.

The train was just pulling in when they arrived at the station, and there was hardly time to call out a thank you to Joanne Taruskin as they raced to catch the train. They found seats amid the crush of Saturday commuters and pulled off their wet rain gear for the ride into New York.

"It's just too much!" Jennifer pinched herself. "I mean, is this really happening?"

"I guess so." Polly grinned. "I think it's gotta be fate, Jen," she added.

"Maybe. But we deserve it. And we did work so hard for this," she insisted, suddenly her old serious self.

Polly raised one eyebrow and looked outside at the rain splashing in diagonal streaks against the window. She glanced at Jennifer's image in the pane of glass and then turned back to her. "Well, I personally feel our guardian angel is really more responsible than all the hard work we put in. Wow, Connecticut in the summer. Do you realize all the guest artists who teach master classes there? Erik Bruhn and Jerome Robbins and maybe even Nureyev!"

"Oh, God!" Jennifer clutched her head in her hands. "What would I say to Nureyev?"

"You wouldn't say anything, dummy, you'd just dance your brains out."

"Boy, a whole summer away from home and parents," Jennifer said, then sighed. "It'll be so different. Poor Andy'll probably pine away to nothing."

Suddenly Polly's throat tightened into a big lump. She hadn't thought about that. What would her mother do all alone for a whole summer? The house felt too big even when the two of them were there. And then once again, she thought about Cott. Not that things were really serious enough between them yet to worry about leaving him for the summer. Since the Harvest

Ball and the afternoon of the eggcreams, they'd only gone out once, to see a revival of *Gone With the Wind*, but they'd been talking on the phone almost every night. Funny, she and Jen used to spend hours on the telephone every day after school, but they hadn't been doing that at all lately. When Cott called her, she felt she could get close to him without actually having the pressure of dating. It felt good—comfortable—and it was really nice to see that he was less boastful and didn't put on his know-it-all act on the phone with her.

"Grand Central *Stay-shee-un!*" called the conductor. The train entered the long tunnel before the last stop and the girls began gathering up their things.

"Do you think there'll still be seats for a Baryshnikov performance?" Jennifer's anxious voice jerked Polly out of her daydream about Cott. She had been imagining how great it would be if he could come up on weekends all through the summer, and after performances they would sit somewhere together and be very quiet and look at the moon.

"I guess. We can get them far in advance." Polly followed the line of people toward the door of the train.

"Do you realize, Polly," Jennifer mused as she took her place behind her, "someday, if we work very hard and dance madly for these two summers, we could end up maybe even dancing with Misha himself! Oh!" The notion was so incredible that she had to steady herself on the back of one of the train seats. "Our whole lives, working together and getting famous, Polly!" she exclaimed.

"I'm glad you have it all worked out." Polly grinned as she steered Jennifer out the door and past the exit from Track 23 to the subway. "But is it okay if *I* pick out what I want for lunch today?"

"Polly!" Jennifer grimaced. "I just meant—"

"I know what you meant. Our whole lives in ballet." She sighed, thinking of Mme Mishkin's speech about how commitment was the most important thing for a dancer. But on the subway up to class, all she could think of was that she had to get to a phone and call Cott.

Mme Mishkin practically genuflected when they walked into the studio. No matter that they were nearly an hour late. They had, in her mind, become larger than life, more precious than gold.

She rapped her time stick on the floor to call the rest of the class to attention. "Mesdemoiselles, plees! An acknowlechment for our winners!" The fifteen girls at the barre stopped their work momentarily, and a smattering of applause ran down the row. Dawn Sims walked over to the rosin box and began rubbing her ballet slippers in it. Polly felt horribly embarrassed.

Mme Mishkin took each of them by the arm. Then, ceremoniously, she kissed first Jennifer and then Polly on both cheeks. "Thees is the result of many goot years, but only the beginning of many more."

Polly could feel it coming. Lecture Number 792 on "grave responsibility." But she was pleasantly surprised when instead, she pushed them toward the barre and told them she would see them later in her private office. Dawn looked away when Polly came to stand next to her, and even when Jennifer began humming along with Joey's rendition of Tchaikovsky's "Waltz of the Flowers" Dawn refused to look at either of them. Polly couldn't help imagining how miserable Dawn must be feeling, but she also knew she and Jennifer deserved their scholarships and had a right to be proud.

When she lined up behind Jennifer for the turns across the floor, she decided she would call Cott as soon as class was over.

The rain had almost stopped when they straggled out of the school at two o'clock, tired but happy. They began walking up Broadway toward Lincoln Center. Polly found it difficult to just walk—every impulse told her to skip, or maybe fly. She looked down at her reflection in the puddle at her feet and decided that today at least, she felt beautiful. That might all change tomorrow, but right now, she was definitely pretty.

"You know," Jennifer mused, walking along on light feet, "I thought I was just going to collapse when I saw Dawn's face today. Was she ever green."

"I know. I guess it's even harder for her because two of us won. She did work hard, after all." Polly was trying her utmost to think of something nice to say about Dawn. She decided it was only right to be generous today.

"Hard, schmard." Jennifer shrugged. "I have *no* sympathy. She's been so mean. Want something to eat?" Jennifer asked absently, stopping to peer into the window of Ballet Makers at an old portrait of Pavlova.

"Not much. Believe it or not, I'm not hungry. I am fed by my Muse." Polly laughed, throwing out her arms and nearly hitting a passerby.

"Wow, wasn't she gorgeous?" Jennifer stared at the Pavlova print.

"Come on, it's starting to rain again." Polly pulled her along Broadway and up the long flight of steps into the plaza of Lincoln Center. Just as the skies opened, they got to the huge doors of the Metropolitan Opera House, where the dancers of American Ballet Theatre performed.

"Whew!" Jennifer exclaimed, racing inside. "Close call." The big drops spattered off the fountain in the center of the plaza, and large spreading lakes began to form all over the cement walk. "Boy, we may have to sleep here tonight," Jennifer said, giggling, but when she turned around, she saw Polly walking purposefully down the corridor.

"Hey, the box office is that way." Running to catch up with her, Jennifer pointed in the opposite direction.

"I know. I just want to make a phone call first," Polly explained. "You go check the programs and see what looks wonderful. I'll be right there."

"Okay," Jennifer agreed, somewhat puzzled. Who was Polly phoning? Probably her mom, she figured as she walked over to the big schedule board next to the box office and wedged herself between several other people to get close to it.

Polly closed the hinged door of the phone booth, and the light went on. She fumbled in her purse for change and then dialed the number she knew by heart. The operator came on, and Polly inserted the required amount in the slot.

The phone rang four times. "Oh, please be home!" Polly muttered under her breath. She brushed a few raindrops off the top of her head, glancing at the ghostly Polly facing her in the door of the phone booth. Her image seemed pretty disheveled. *Good thing we don't have video telephones yet,* she thought.

"Hello," said a woman's voice on the other end.

"Hello. Is Cott there?" Polly asked anxiously.

"Just a moment, please."

While she waited, Polly fiddled with the quarters, dimes, and nickels she had placed on the ledge in front of her and was very relieved when Cott picked up.

"Cott Townsend," he responded in a very proper, well-bred voice.

"Hi," Polly said shyly. "It's me."

"Pol, how're you doin'!" Cott's manner loosened up at once as he realized who it was. "Where are you? You sound far away."

"The City. I have ballet on Saturdays, remember?"

"Oh yeah, right. You going to be around later today?" he asked hopefully.

"Maybe. But listen," she burst out, unable to remain cool a second longer. "I have *great* news. I won—I mean, we won! Both Jennifer and I." She was smiling again as she told him.

"Pol! That's fantastic! Of course I knew all along you'd be the one. No one else could have a chance next to you. Oh, except Jennifer, I guess," he added. "So tell me all about it."

She sat back and leaned against the side of the booth. "Well, we go to Connecticut at the end of June for the next two summers, and we take class with all the greats—not just ballet but modern, jazz, ethnic, mime, everything. And we perform constantly. And they give us room and board and maybe even a four-year college scholarship after that. Boy, is my mother going to hit the ceiling when she hears!" she raced on, suddenly thinking of her mother's continual complaints about paying for Polly's dancing lessons.

"Hey, this is terrific," Cott exclaimed on the other end. "There's only one terrible thing about it."

"What? What are you talking about?"

At that moment, the connection was interrupted, and the operator's mechanical voice demanded more money.

"Give me your number," Cott offered. "I'll call you back."

"It's—um, 212 924-7377," Polly read off, dropping one dime into the slot to appease the anonymous voice, "but sometimes it doesn't work when you call a pay phone. If we get cut off, I'll call you from the station as soon as we pull into Mamaroneck."

"I'll pick you up," he insisted. "We're going to celebrate tonight. Champagne, roses, sweaty leotards, you name it. Anyway, hang up. Let me call you back."

Polly, laughing out loud, put the receiver back on the hook and sat back to wait. She expected the phone to ring instantly, but it didn't. She waited impatiently. What should she do? she wondered. She hadn't even told him what train she'd be on. Should she call him back?

Just then the phone rang. She picked it up instantly. "Hi," she said breathlessly, then went on, not waiting for him to respond. "What happened?"

"I was so excited about your news that I dialed the wrong number," Cott said. "Anyway, where were we?"

"You still haven't told me what's so awful about my winning this scholarship."

"Hey, babe, don't you know I'm gonna miss you like crazy?" Cott asked, his voice sounding very hurt.

Polly looked at the phone receiver as though it had just turned into something alive. "Well, I—you can visit. I mean, I hope you will."

"If I'm around," he said slowly. "My dad's been talking about either Europe or the Coast this summer."

"Oh." Polly's bright bubble seemed to be getting smaller. "That would be—" She heard a tap on the glass and looked up. Jennifer was standing before her, her hands on her hips, looking annoyed. Polly swung the door half open. "Just a sec."

"Polly, I've been examining that board for so long I could perform most of those ballets myself by now!"

"I—just a minute!" She closed the door and said to Cott, "Look, I've gotta go."

70

"What train are you taking back?"

"I guess the four-twenty. You'll be there?"

"I'll be there," he promised. "Bye."

"Bye." She replaced the receiver on its cradle and swung the door open to greet a very disgruntled Jennifer.

"You certainly took long enough," she muttered, starting back down the corridor. "Who was that?"

"Cott." Polly stuck her purse back in the zippered compartment of her knapsack and walked along slowly beside her friend.

"Why'd you call him now?"

Polly stopped and made an exasperated face at her. "To tell him it's raining," she said sarcastically. "Really, Jennifer! I wanted him to know about our winning. What else?"

"It could have waited. I haven't called Andy yet." She was studying the schedule board as though she were trying to memorize it. Actually, Polly hadn't told her about all the late-night phone conversations with Cott, and she didn't know anything more about their relationship other than that they had had one movie date.

"Well, that's where you and I are different," Polly said. "So what do you want to see?"

"You choose," she said disinterestedly. "They're all good."

"For heaven's sake, Jennifer!"

"What?" Jennifer's eyes were all scrunched

up as she regarded Polly, a sure sign that she was feeling neglected and upset.

"Just because I called him, you're acting like—I don't know. Like you're jealous."

Jennifer's mouth flew open in astonishment. "Oh, don't be absurd. You can be so stupid sometimes."

Polly realized that they were standing in the way of several couples waiting to buy tickets, and she was suddenly embarrassed. You couldn't just leave a conversation like this in the air, but you couldn't really hold up traffic either. "Hey," she suggested. "let's get our seats and then discuss this."

"There is nothing to discuss!" Jennifer nearly yelled, stalking away to stand on line. "I'd like the December third or tenth performance, if that's okay with you. Misha's only dancing at night, so we'll have to break Mom's rule about the matinee."

"Sure." Polly wondered miserably whether they'd still be talking on December third or tenth. Maybe Cott would have some idea about how to handle this.

When they reached the head of the line, they pushed their money under the little barred window in exchange for their tickets. The skinny young man behind the counter filtered Polly's single dollar bills through his fingers disdainfully, as if to say that people who bought tickets at this theater only paid with large bills. The girls wandered off to the side and checked their numbers against the seating plan before starting for the big glass doors leading to Lincoln Center plaza.

"Seems to have stopped," Polly said. The puddles lay scattered everywhere. A little boy was jumping from one to the next as they went outside. Without speaking, the girls walked over to the subway stop and down the stairs to buy their tokens.

"I guess we can make the four-twenty," Polly said anxiously, looking at her watch. Above all, she didn't want to say anything about Cott picking her up. Probably Jennifer wouldn't even fit in the back of his MG, and she'd have to call her mother to come get her while Polly rode off in style. Oh, this was awful. Why couldn't she have a best friend and a boyfriend both at the same time?

The ride home was quiet, filled with a lot of tension and unspoken thoughts. Polly tried to concentrate on the historical romance she was reading, but her mind kept wandering. When the girls got off the train and stepped onto the platform, Jennifer saw Cott's car first. That did it.

"Oh, I see," she said indignantly. "I didn't know you had a date."

"I—uh, well, he just said he'd pick us up," Polly explained lamely. She felt soggy inside and out. As she watched Cott jump out of his car and run toward them, she thought about the fairness of things and how unbalanced life really was. This morning, she and Jennifer had been as close as sisters, or lifelong partners. Now there seemed to be a wide gulf between them.

Chapter Five

"Oops, sorry!" Polly banged the door of her gym locker back into Jennifer's.

"Why don't you watch—? Hey, that's a *super* dress." Jennifer nodded approvingly. She watched her friend tear off her gym clothes and throw a black-watch plaid shirtwaist over her head. She put on forest green sheer pantyhose to match and low-heeled black pumps. She was dressing as though someone had just announced that the building was on fire.

"Thanks," she gasped, running her fingers through her short hair to fluff it up. She nearly barged right into Barbara Moffat, who was trying to get a look at herself in the full-length mirror at the same time.

"Polly!" Barbara yelled when she was nearly jabbed by a bony elbow.

Jennifer walked over to the mirror. She had a puzzled expression on her face. "Would you mind very much if I asked you a question?" She pursed her lips and regarded Polly, who was about to fly off in several directions.

"Sure. What?" Polly gasped, throwing her deodorant and cologne into her gym bag. Then she thought better of it and pulled off the top of the cologne bottle so she could douse herself with it once again.

"Where are you rushing off to now, why are you so dressed up on a school day, and *where* is your head?" Jennifer ticked the items off on her fingers.

"I—uh, I'm going to the City."

"With Cott?" Jennifer asked softly. She already knew the answer.

"Yup. I'm late. Bye." Polly thrust her bag back in her locker, whisked up her books and purse, and was halfway out the door of the gym before Jennifer caught up with her.

"Polly! Aren't you going to tell me where you're going?" Jennifer pouted. Her frustrated tone of voice was enough to make Polly stop in her traces. She looked at her friend, still dressed in her Mamaroneck High T-shirt and baggie shorts, and she realized she was being really rude.

Since she had started going out with Cott, she just hadn't had time for all the things she and Jennifer used to do together. In the old days, they had spent every single afternoon dancing or doing homework or just fooling around, and they usually had dinner at each other's houses at least three times a week. Then there were the evenings at the mall or going to a movie with either Mrs. Luria or the Taruskins. It had been a whole routine, a way of life, even. Polly suddenly had this sinking feeling in the center of her chest. *What am I doing?* she asked herself, focusing on Jennifer's long blond braid. She just couldn't look into her eyes.

"Sorry. Sure I want to tell you." Girls were racing madly out of the locker room, free from gym and Friday's final period. "Cott and I are going to the Library of the Performing Arts at Lincoln Center. Then he's taking me to dinner and the ballet."

"Oh." Jennifer was trying hard not to show how left out she felt. Polly hadn't even mentioned this to her before. "Listen, have a great time. See you at the train tomorrow before class. You—ah—you are coming to class?" She was slowly pulling her T-shirt over her head.

"Naturally. I couldn't miss ballet, silly." Polly yanked Jennifer's braid and grabbed her trench coat from its hook. She started for the door again.

"Have fun." Jennifer's voice sounded awfully far away. Polly ran from the sound of it, down the stairs and out the front door of Mamaroneck High. She was still thinking about how forlorn Jennifer seemed when Cott appeared at her side.

"Boy, do you look nice!" He grinned, taking off his glasses to admire her. Then, to get a better look at her face, he came very close and squinted myopically. She could smell the light scent of his after-shave.

"Thanks." She smiled shyly. "You, too." He had on gray slacks and a black blazer with silver buttons that had some kind of crest hammered into them. She wondered if maybe it was a family crest, if maybe somewhere far back, his ancestors had been dukes or earls. Townsend was a pretty classy-sounding name. A lot more interesting than Luria, she mused as he walked her to his car. Although Taruskin had a very nice ring to it. Then, thinking of Jennifer again, she was suddenly sad.

"How was your day?" Cott flung open the door on the passenger side and helped her into the tiny car. She loved the feel of sinking back into the plush red leather bucket seats.

"It was okay," she said, snuggling down and wrapping her coat around her. "Got an A in that spot French quiz."

"Hey, terrific," he said, putting the key into the ignition and setting the MG's motor humming. Cott had a special feeling for French, having spent several summers in Provence when he was small. He was always promising to show her the Eiffel Tower someday, a notion that made her heart beat a lot faster. One part of Polly told herself firmly that Cott loved to exaggerate; the other part told her that he really meant it, because since the day she'd convinced him that he didn't have to boast or brag to impress her, he had always been totally straight with her. When he offered to take her to Paris, it was like any other guy offering to take her to a movie.

"Yeah, I was pretty knocked out." She smiled. "I did what you suggested the other night on the phone."

"What'd I say?"

"To recite the conjugations to music while I did my warm-up. Kinda catchy, you know, '*je parle, tu parles, il parle . . .*' cha, cha, cha."

"You're pretty funny." He laughed as they sped down the highway to Manhattan. "Not to mention pretty *pretty*."

Polly blushed and looked over at him. In the weeks that they'd been talking on the phone and doing things together, they'd only had four honest-to-goodness dates, and this was the first time they'd gone into the City. But the nice thing about it was that Polly never felt that yukky better-be-on-your-toes-because-you're-out-with-a-boy sensation that she'd always had with boys before. Cott was different—he was easy to be with.

"Hello, are you there?" He was looking over at her, an amused expression on his face.

"Sorry, I guess I just . . . faded out for a second." She was terribly embarrassed to have been caught daydreaming, and again, she thought of Jennifer. Naturally, she couldn't tell

Cott what she'd been thinking, and she had always shared all her dreams with her best friend. *Up until now*, she reminded herself, remembering the scene in the locker room that afternoon.

"Sometimes, when I have to spend a 'family evening' at home, I do the same thing," Cott confessed, laughing. "You know, my dad's going on about how lousy the market is, and my stepmom is telling him how the manicurist nearly ruined her nails, and I just go away." He took one hand off the steering wheel and made a running motion in the air with his fingers.

"Where do you go?" Polly asked earnestly. When she and her mom spent time alone, they were always talking.

"You know, my brain just does other things. Let's see," he said, "I try to remember Beatles' lyrics, or I think about this trip I really want to take where I'll stay up all night and watch the animals in Kenya, or sometimes, lately, I think about you."

Polly couldn't speak, she was so surprised. She was more pleased about Cott telling her this than she'd ever been about anything in her life except winning the scholarship, and the only words her lips were actually able to form were, "Do you think we'll find a parking space?" She could have kicked herself.

* * *

The library was filled with recordings of such greats as Bix Beiderbecke, King Oliver, Bessie Smith, and Louis Armstrong. Polly put on earphones to listen to a Django Reinhardt record, and she stood mesmerized by the incredible riffs that slid off the musician's guitar. She'd never heard anything like this before. Actually, she knew nothing at all about jazz and very little about music in general. Her repertoire of composers was limited to Tchaikovsky and Chopin for ballet class, and the Stones and Steely Dan for everything else. That was about it.

Cott came over and watched her for a minute, saw her foot tapping unself-consciously in time to the cool, rhythmic melodies. As the piece ended, she turned to him, a wide smile on her face.

"Like that?" Cott took the headphones off her and ruffled her hair lightly to put it back in its tousled shape.

"He's fantastic, unbelievable! God, I'd love to dance to that. Not ballet, but you know, something more interpretive."

He ignored the stupefied looks of the other people in the library and executed a perfect time-step. "Baby, I *know* what you are talking *about*." He stopped dancing, and together they walked sedately past the guard and out the front door.

"I've got a whole collection of vintage jazz at

home. Believe it or not, my miserable old father got me started on it. We don't have a lot in common," Cott said somewhat bitterly, "but music soothes both us savage beasts. Hey!" His eyes suddenly lit up with a new idea. "How about we don't go to the ballet? Let's go order a pizza and just sit around and listen to records at my father's New York apartment."

Polly bit her lip. "Will—ah—he be there?" she asked. As much as she liked Cott, she wasn't sure they'd known each other long enough to spend a whole evening alone listening to records.

"Sure. He lives there during the week. Only sees us on weekends. Big business before family every time!" He rolled his eyes and started pulling Polly toward the phone booth on the corner. I'll call him and tell him we're coming over. Okay?"

"But, the tickets—" She had been looking forward to seeing Nureyev and Carla Fracci the way other girls would anticipate seeing Bruce Springsteen.

"So, we'll do it another time. Unless—" He whirled around and grabbed her by the shoulders. "Now, tell me the truth. Can you bear to spend a whole night just looking at me?"

Polly giggled. "I'll force myself. But you've *bought* the tickets."

"Polly, kiddo, no sweat. See, I'll show you." He walked back to the entrance of the library, where a middle-aged couple stood poring over a map of New York City. The man was short and had thin hair combed down over his forehead, and the woman was clutching her purse to her side as though she knew a mugger was going to accost her at any moment.

Cott cleared his throat and went over to the couple. Curious, Polly sidled up to hear the conversation. What was this madman up to now?

"Excuse me sir, madam?" Cott had his refined telephone voice on, Polly noted, but even so, the woman clutched her handbag even tighter.

"Ah, yes?" The man frowned up at Cott.

"I note that you two must have a certain interest in music"—he gestured toward the imposing buildings of Lincoln Center—"and I was wondering if you like dance as well."

"I—" The man seemed certain that Cott was trying to sell him something.

"Are you folks at all interested in classical ballet? You really shouldn't visit New York without going to the ballet at least once," he went on persuasively.

"Well, I just *love* ballet," the woman gushed.

"Do you?" He looked over at Polly, who was staring at the scene, amazed. "Because I just happen to have two front-row mezzanine seats for tonight that I can't use. My girlfriend and I were really looking forward to it, but my father—he's the mayor—just sent the limousine over for us. The chauffeur's parked right around the corner. See, Dad wants us at Gracie Mansion on the double, because there are some very important foreign dignitaries coming to dinner. He says we just have to be there." He looked at his watch.

"Your father's the mayor of New York?" The woman's purse was instantly at ease, although she still seemed very much in awe of Cott.

"You mean, that Ed Koch?" the man exclaimed. "I didn't know he was married."

"Funny," the woman said, scrutinizing Cott's handsome face, "you don't really look like him."

"I take after my mother," Cott explained, pressing the tickets into the man's hand.

"Well, I—well, thanks." He smiled and reached into his back pocket for his wallet.

"Oh, no, they're yours," Cott protested, grabbing Polly's hand and pulling her along down the street. She was trying not to choke with laughter.

"Hey, I—hey, thanks!" the man yelled as Cott and Polly ran toward the entrance of the Lincoln Center garage.

"I can't believe you did that!" Polly squealed. Her face was pink from laughing so much. "I am totally dumbfounded. Those seats must have cost—"

"Listen, it's like he got an early Christmas present, right?" Cott reasoned. "People are always griping about how lousy New Yorkers are. I'm out to change the image, that's all."

Polly stopped to stare at him. "You're incred-ible," she murmured.

"You don't really mind, do you?" he asked, suddenly serious. "We'll go to the ballet next week, okay?"

"Sure." Polly was really pleased that he was more concerned about disappointing her than anything else. It wasn't as if he was trying to flaunt his being rich by giving the tickets away—he sort of took wealth for granted. The nicest part of it was that he obviously enjoyed making other people happy. He'd made that couple's evening, and he had enjoyed doing it. Polly thought of the flashy impression he'd first tried to create to get her attention, and she shook her head, smiling. Cott Townsend wasn't like that at all. He was actually pretty terrific.

Cott parked the MG in his father's reserved space on Sutton Place. The townhouse was at the end of a dead-end street, and it had a small terrace overlooking the East River. It was elabo-rately decorated with planters filled to overflow-ing with yellow and white chrysanthemums and yellow-orange marigolds.

"Guess he must have had Jimmy drop him off," Cott murmured, balancing a pepperoni and mushroom pizza in one hand as he reached for his keys with the other.

"Who's Jimmy?" Polly asked, examining the bleached stucco townhouse with black trim. It looked as if it belonged in Southern California instead of New York City.

"Chauffeur. Dad doesn't like to keep the Jaguar down here, so Jimmy just drops him off." He led her into the front hallway, and Polly stood on the marble mosaic tiles, gaping. She knew the Townsends had money, but this was beyond belief. The modern chandelier over her head looked as if it were made of thousands of tiny icicles suspended in the air. As Cott turned up the dimmer, she saw the huge circular living room ahead of them.

They passed the connecting door, which looked like something created in another century, when craftsmen had had time to devote all their attention to making the very best. The slab of oak was inlaid with mother-of-pearl in an intricate geometric pattern. As Polly looked ahead into the living room, she saw that one entire wall was a window looking out on the river and that an imposing Steinway grand piano sat beside it, the centerpiece of the room. The plush, rose-colored carpet gave under her shoes: it was like walking on a fur cushion. The blond wood furniture was all built into the various levels of the room, and although it was extremely functional, it gave off an aura of elegance and comfort. The walls were covered with paintings—Polly recognized a Chagall, a Matisse, and a Picasso. *I wonder if they're originals*, she mused, and then she decided that they probably were.

Cott took her by the hand and led her past the piano into a smaller sitting room. "What's wrong?" he grinned. "You look shell-shocked."

"You might say that," Polly said. She hoped it wasn't in terrible taste to gawk, but she figured she had to be honest with him. She'd simply never seen anything this luxurious.

"Don't worry." Cott smiled as he opened yet another extraordinary door. "They're just material possessions, right? The real me doesn't care about any of this," he confided. Then he raised his voice. "Dad, you home?"

"Up here," came the booming response.

Cott took Polly by both shoulders and held her at arm's length. "Are you ready for this? He won't bite—promise."

"Sure. I'm game."

Cott left their pizza on a porcelain tray on an end table and led her into another hall, where a spiral staircase loomed above them.

"Mr. Townsend will receive you in the study, milady." Cott bowed and snickered, then pointed Polly ahead of him up the winding stairs. She was both nervous and excited about meeting a big TV producer. Ever since Jennifer had discovered who Cott's father was, she had started a list. Whenever she saw his name in the credits on a show, she wrote it down for Polly.

"Come right in," said the deep voice Polly had

heard downstairs. She took the last three steps up and found herself in the middle of a mahogany-paneled study, as dark as the living room was light. Small brass carriage lamps shone from the walls around the room. At the far end, sitting behind a gigantic wood and leather desk, was an attractive, tanned man in his late forties with short steel-gray hair and a salt-and-pepper mustache. His tie was undone around his neck, and his shirt-sleeves were rolled up. When Polly walked in, he glanced at her over his half-glasses.

"Hi, how are you?" he asked casually, not bothering to get up.

"Ah, fine thanks. And you?" Polly responded shyly.

"Hi, Mitch." Cott walked up the stairs behind her and gently pushed her forward. "This is Polly Luria. Polly, Mitch Townsend."

Polly walked over to take the man's outstretched hand, wondering whether Cott had always called his father by his first name. It seemed like a really California thing to do.

"So, you kids go to school together, huh?" He seemed very eager to get back to work.

"Right. We thought we'd just listen to some of the old records, if it won't hassle you too much." Cott, seemingly unconcerned about having interrupted his father's work, was playing with an antique camera that was perched on its stand in a corner of the room. Polly kept thinking she wished she'd had her raincoat cleaned for this occasion.

"Yeah, fine. I'm just catching up on the production costs for the Bacall special. If you guys don't mind—" He indicated the printouts spread all over his desk.

"We'll be down in the living room." Cott suddenly looked annoyed. "Sorry to bother you." He came back to Polly and led her to the staircase, but just before he started down the steps, she noticed a softer look come into his eyes. He turned back toward his father. "We got a large pizza, Mitch. In case you want some."

"What? Oh, no thanks. Darya said if I missed her ten o'clock supper one more time she'd divorce me." He gave a short laugh. "Say, as long as you're here—yeah, that's a good idea— would you and—ah, Polly—it *is* Polly?"

"Yes," she answered quietly.

"Well, I have these comps here. That new Wexler musical opening in a few weeks. Darya and I are going to be on the Coast, so why don't you two use them? It's for opening night and the cast party afterward."

He reached into the inside pocket of the jacket sitting behind him over the arms of his tall chair. "I hear it's supposed to be the smash hit of the season," he said, getting up and coming toward them. Polly looked at him closely as he walked across the room. He and Cott could almost have passed for brothers. Mr. Townsend was just as tall and in very good physical shape. *Probably works out at a gym,* Polly decided.

"Well, thanks, Mitch. December tenth," Cott said, examining the tickets. He smiled at Polly. "This kinda makes up for the ones we got rid of earlier, huh? Sounds good to me; how about you?"

She nodded. "Thanks, Mr. Townsend. I'm sure we'll enjoy it," she said politely. How awkward Cott seemed with his father. It was as if they didn't know each other very well.

"So, you guys going to be back for Christmas?" Cott asked casually, starting down the stairs.

"Probably. Definitely New Year's. You kids bring anyone you want for the midnight bash. Well, I'll leave you to your pizza. Nice to meet you, ah—Polly. Polly."

"You, too, Mr. Townsend." As Polly walked back down the stairs behind a rather disgruntled-looking Cott, she couldn't help thinking that money wasn't everything. It sure wasn't a replacement for not having Christmas with your family. No wonder Cott acted the way he did sometimes.

"So," Cott said brightly when they were down the stairs, "let's get that vinyl spinning! You dish out the pizza."

Chapter Six

"December tenth! You're not serious!" Jennifer was sewing a run in her pink tights when Polly broke the news, and she nearly rammed the needle through her finger.

"Why? What's wrong now?" Polly had been enthusiastically regaling Jennifer with the story of her date with Cott and meeting Mitchell Townsend when her friend suddenly blew up.

"Polly." Jennifer stuck the needle in the top of the waistband and sucked on her injured finger. "Perhaps you do not recall the day we won our scholarships."

"Huh? Of course I—"

"And perhaps," Jennifer rushed on, "you don't remember going to Lincoln Center with me and buying tickets to the performance of *La Bayadère*? The date was December tenth."

"Oh, no!" Polly wailed. She sat down heavily

next to Jennifer on the sofa in the Taruskin living room.

"Yes." Jennifer primly pursed her lips and started sewing again, jabbing the needle through the rip beside the seam as though she were sawing wood.

"But I have to go with Cott. It's—it's a Broadway opening." Polly seemed stunned. How could she have forgotten the date? Where was her brain lately? And what was she going to do now?

"Well, bully for Broadway."

"Listen, you—you can have my ticket. You could ask Andy to go with you."

"Oh, that's *real* fine." Jennifer ran the thread backward through the mended area, then tied a tight double knot. "I'm supposed to invite Andy to the ballet? Andy, who probably thinks Nijinsky is some kind of Russian food!" She got up and walked across the room, glaring at the furniture instead of at Polly.

"I'm sorry," Polly murmured. "I don't know what else to say." She wrapped herself deeper into her bulky Irish-knit sweater and leaned back against the sofa cushions. Suddenly she was chilled, although the November evening was very mild.

Jennifer turned to face her. "You could say you'd tell him you have a prior engagement."

"I—"

"But you won't. You think your boyfriend is

more important. He's just *the* most important thing in the world!"

"That's not true!" Polly exploded, jumping off the couch to go to Jennifer. "You're my best friend. You're—"

"I'm not a damn boy!" Her blue eyes were swimming with tears as she looked into Polly's face. "Maybe I'm being difficult and unreasonable, but frankly, I don't think so. I think you have your priorities all mixed up." She walked to the living room door. "I'm really sorry, but I have lots to do. I promised Mom I'd help her with the turkey stuffing." She spat the words at Polly and stalked out of the room.

Polly stood there for a second before going to the hall closet to get her down jacket. She peered at her reflection in the mirror above the little rickety table that held letters, hats, gloves, and an assortment of change.

What kind of person are you? she asked the Polly in the mirror. She was so guilty she could feel the hot shame behind her eyes. *You used to be nice and considerate. Now you're just boy-crazy. A totally typical teenager.*

She bit her lip and wondered whether she should tell Cott she couldn't go with him on the tenth. But maybe he'd never ask her out again if she broke this date. Of course, if he was that kind of guy, who wouldn't understand her forgetting that she'd had a date with Jennifer, then maybe she didn't want anything more to do with him.

Now just hold on. Why are you blaming Cott for this? It's your own dumb fault. She sighed and pulled her white wool cap over her rumpled hair. Just as she was pulling open the door, she was surprised by a voice right behind her. It was Mrs. Taruskin.

"Oh, Polly, are you going? I thought you were sticking around to help us with the Thanksgiving preparations."

"Ah, sorry, I've just . . . I really have to get home."

"Oh, all right." Mrs. Taruskin shrugged and flicked a piece of lint off her navy blue cardigan. "I suppose we'll see you tomorrow then."

"I'll try." Polly was practically sobbing, and she made her escape as quickly as she could without seeming awfully rude. She rushed into the front yard and ran for her bicycle.

"Are you sure you wouldn't rather have Dr. Taruskin drive you?" Joanne Taruskin called to her in a concerned tone.

"No, thanks," Polly managed to say, throwing her leg over the bike seat and pedaling furiously down the drive. She just *had* to get out of there. When she was home, in her own room, maybe she'd be able to think more clearly.

"What's wrong with Polly?" asked Mrs. Taruskin as she walked into the kitchen. Using a hand chopper, Jennifer was wildly mashing up the chestnuts for the stuffing.

"Oh, I guess she must have her period," she muttered. "Where do you want these?" She indicated the bowl of raisins soaking in Southern Comfort.

"Just throw them in with the bread crumbs, dear," said Mrs. Taruskin. She busied herself getting pots from under the sink. "You did ask Mrs. Luria personally to come over for cake and coffee after they get back from their Thanksgiving?"

"Um." Jennifer scooped all the ingredients together in a big bowl and stirred them with a wooden spoon.

"Was that a yes or a no? Jennifer?" Puzzled, she came over and stood before her daughter. She was even more confused when she saw two large tears creeping down Jennifer's face. "Dear, what is it? What's the matter?"

"Nothing." Jennifer looked down into the bowl, concentrating hard on one particular piece of chestnut.

"You don't have to talk about it," her mother said softly. "But it might help. I've noticed things have been sort of strained between you girls lately."

Jennifer nodded and took a seat at the kitchen table. "It's just—well, we were always together. We told each other everything, you know. We did everything together."

"I know, dear, but—"

"And now she's acting like a dumb idiot with that—that *rich* kid." Jennifer said "rich" as though it were a dirty word.

"Is that the Cott she's always talking about?"

"Yeah. And *I* was the one who got them together."

Mrs. Taruskin sat beside her daughter and looked at her thoughtfully. "Sweetheart, it happens to everyone. To all of us. You grow up, and you have a boyfriend, and you feel special about him."

"Listen," Jennifer said fiercely, "I have a boyfriend—sort of—and he doesn't make me act like a romantic robot. I don't do stupid things like letting my friends down."

"Jennifer, darling," her mother said, smiling, "when you really feel strongly about a boy, your interests change. That's part of growing up. You change your allegiances as you get older so that one day you can make a real commitment to a man and get married. Polly is—well, she's just a bit more mature than you, that's all," she finished.

Jennifer slammed the wooden spoon down, scattering raisins around the table. "That's a real old-fashioned attitude, Mom. I don't buy it. Friends are friends until they stop caring. And that goes for boys *or* girls." She ran from the room and didn't stop, racing past the doorway of the den, where her sister and father were reading quietly. She rushed upstairs and into her bedroom, throwing herself flat across the quilted bedspread. She couldn't cry because she was holding her breath. She only hoped that Polly was home by now, doing exactly the same thing.

Polly wasn't really sure how she banged up her toe, she told Cott on the phone Thanksgiving night. She and her mother had driven to New Jersey to her aunt's house for the holiday, and just as she was on her way down the front porch steps to leave, she had tripped and fallen flat on her face. Naturally, it had to be the badly healed broken toe—it throbbed like anything, and the least touch caused her to yelp.

But Polly did know why it happened. Ever since she had realized what she had done to Jennifer, she just hadn't been thinking. She couldn't even walk down a set of porch steps.

"I'll come right over," Cott offered. "I'll make you an ice pack."

"Already got one." Polly laughed. "My mother loves to mother me." She eased herself back against the headboard and switched the phone to her other shoulder.

"Hey, we've got to get you all well in time for the New Year's party," Cott insisted. "I promised Mitch you'd dance for him."

"You did not."

"Sure. He's always eager to meet a rising young star."

"Cott, he probably doesn't even remember me." Polly smiled to herself, thinking back to that evening in Mr. Townsend's apartment.

"Yeah, well, he has trouble remembering me sometimes, too," Cott said sarcastically.

"Cott—"

"Listen, it's a real drag over here. The *grown-ups* are all turkey-ed out. And my sister, who's down from Vassar, is busy showing off her rock."

"Rock?"

"Her diamond. She's engaged to this big banker type. He and Mitch have so much in common you'd think they both learned to talk inside the New York Stock Exchange."

Polly sighed. She was glad that he wanted to be with her so much, but it was clear that he also wanted to get away from something else. As the days went by and they got together after school or on weekends, Polly found new and different things to like about Cott. He certainly was less cranky than Jennifer, and even though she couldn't share the same things with him as she did with her best friend—like ballet or family get-togethers—he was very supportive of her and cared a lot about how she felt.

Polly realized that she was continually comparing Jennifer and Cott: the new, strong feelings she had for him were not the familiar, cozy ones she had for her friend. And she was finding it difficult to give both Jennifer and Cott the proper amount of attention. Sometimes she got very nervous wondering if she'd ever have to give one up for the other, but she tried not to think about that too often. It was too depressing.

"Well, you can't really come over now because my mother and I are on our way to the Taruskins for a post-Thanksgiving celebration."

"Could I—would it be okay if I came with you?"

Polly was surprised at the vulnerable tone in his voice. *Poor guy,* she thought, *he must really hate being with his folks.*

"I can't see why not. I think you'd like the Taruskins."

"I like *you.* So hold on, I'll be there in five."

When he arrived in the MG, Mrs. Luria absolutely refused to let Polly ride on the back ledge, so they all piled into the Toyota and got to the Taruskins' just before a light smattering of snow began to hit the ground and then dissolve.

Polly and Cott climbed up the front steps as Mrs. Luria went to the trunk of the car for an umbrella. Polly rang the bell. "The first snow, wow. I always love that," she said as they waited.

Before Cott could respond the door flew open. "Why are you never, ever on time?" Jennifer complained. Her face changed as she saw Cott standing in the shadows.

"I—oh, Jennifer, I hope this is okay. Cott was

sort of—well, he asked if he could come. I didn't think you'd mind."

"Mind? Of course not," Jennifer said primly, opening the door all the way. She looked wonderful in a cherry red sweater dress, but from the pinched, unhappy expression on Jennifer's face, Polly knew immediately that she'd made a mistake.

"Hi! How are you both?" gushed Mrs. Taruskin, welcoming Polly's mother at the door with a big kiss.

"I hope this will be all right, Joanne. We brought you an extra guest. This is Cott Townsend."

"Thanks for having me, Mrs. Taruskin," Cott said, smiling warmly and extending his hand. Polly noticed that Jennifer had gone promptly to the kitchen to do whatever busywork she could get her hands on. *Oh, why don't I think!* she asked herself miserably as Mrs. Taruskin ushered her into the living room. Two groups of relatives were sitting on opposite sides of the room, noisily playing a game of charades.

"Now, Polly and Jane, you stay on our side, and Cott, you can be on Jennifer's team," she said just as Jennifer emerged from the kitchen with a big tray of cookies and coffeecake. "My husband is attempting to show us all what's what. Go ahead, dear."

There were two places left to sit down after Polly wedged herself in next to Jennifer's Aunt

Adele on the sofa. The only other seats were on a big cushion on the floor on the opposite side of the room, next to Nancy Taruskin's chair. So after Cott plopped himself down to watch Dr. Taruskin's antics, Jennifer had no choice other than to sit down next to him. Polly held her breath and looked directly at her best friend, but Jennifer refused to look back.

"Okay, okay," Joanne Taruskin's mother, Mrs. Sidler, called. "Get on with it, Bob."

The doctor wound up his hands like film reels and squinted through an imaginary camera.

"Movie title!" Cott called out.

He nodded happily and bent over as though he were leaning on a crutch.

"Old movie! What kind, Bob?" Mrs. Sidler demanded.

He thought for a second, then made a horrible face and waved clawlike fingers at Jennifer. "Horror movie!" she screamed.

"Okay." Nancy ticked the elements off on her right hand. "We've established that it's the title of an old horror film."

"Good, Nancy," Jennifer said sarcastically.

Bob Taruskin held up one finger, then three fingers.

"First word. Three-word title." Cott grinned.

The doctor ran over to his wife and scooped her out of her chair, plastering her hands together in front of her as though she were praying. Then he smoothed imaginary fabric down her back and out behind her, holding it up like a train of a long gown.

"Queen!" yelled Mrs. Sidler.

"Wedding," called Jane Luria.

"I know!" Nancy Taruskin bounced out of her chair, her serious face shining. "I've got it! 'Member of the Wedding'!"

Jennifer gave her a look. "That is not a horror film, Nancy."

"Oh. Oh, yeah," she admitted, settling back in her seat.

Dr. Taruskin was still fiddling with his wife's imaginary dress, and Cott suddenly snapped his fingers. "Not wedding!" he proclaimed. "Bride!"

"Sure!" Jennifer chimed in as her father nodded vehemently. Then he held up two fingers.

"Second word. Little word."

"In! No—of!" Jennifer shouted.

" 'Bride of Frankenstein,' " Cott declared, thumping his partner on the shoulder.

"That's it," Dr. Taruskin breathed, easing himself back into his chair. "I thought I was going to have to be Elsa Lanchester for a minute there." He wiped his brow. "I sure could use some coffee."

"I'll get it, Dad," Jennifer said laughing. She stood and started for the kitchen.

"I'll help," Cott offered, following her. Polly looked up, astounded. Just before Cott walked out of the room, he turned and winked at Polly.

"How's your toe feeling, dear?" Polly's mother came over and squeezed her hand.

"It's fine, Mom," Polly said, smiling. "Everything's fine."

"Here Polly and Jennifer go spinning around like dervishes all the time and never hurt themselves, and then she tries to destroy her feet on stairs and roller skates." Polly's mother went over to Jennifer's mother to commiserate.

"Don't I know. It's a good thing the girls have one another to look after," Joanne murmured. "Now where's that coffee?"

"I'll go see," Polly said decisively. She was absolutely dying to know how her best friend and her boyfriend were getting along. "Be right back." She limped slowly to the kitchen door and hesitated a second before pushing it open. Jennifer was measuring spoonfuls of coffee into the pot and was totally convulsed in giggles.

"So then he says, 'You canna come ina here unlessa you say sworda-feesh.' "

Jennifer gulped with laughter. "Oh, stop, please! I'll spill the hot water. Oh, hi, Polly." She turned, still laughing, to look at Polly, who was wearing an expression of utter astonishment on her face.

"He does the greatest Chico Marx!" Jennifer explained.

"Just showing off again," Cott said quietly to Polly. It was almost an apology.

"Cott's going to lend us his advanced placement English notes from last year," Jennifer went on, wiping the tears of laughter from her eyes.

"That's—it's terrific. Thanks," Polly nodded to him, coming to his side. She understood immediately that without saying anything to him, Cott had fathomed all the problems between her and Jennifer—and between himself and Jennifer. In his own way, he was doing his best to tell Jennifer he really wasn't the louse she thought he was.

"Oh, and I invited Jennifer and Andy to the New Year's Eve party. She says she'll come if she gets to taste caviar and meet my father."

"It's a deal," Jennifer said, pouring water over the coffee grounds. Polly was stunned. She couldn't think of a thing to say, while these two were talking away as though they'd been friends for years.

"Come on, you," Jennifer said, pushing the tray with the sugar and cream into Polly's hands. "We have to figure out what we're going to wear. New Year's on Sutton Place, wow."

She pushed Polly ahead of her out of the room, and just before they walked back into the noisy living room, she whispered in her ear, "I still think it's a terrible thing you did, deciding to break our date, but I gotta hand it to you, he's fabulous."

Polly whirled around, forgetting all about her toe and wincing as she stepped hard on it. "I'm really happy you're getting along," she whispered back.

"Me, too," Jennifer nodded, and then they went in to join the adults.

Chapter Seven

The four of them stood outside in the cold on Sutton Place. "Everybody ready?" Cott asked.

"I certainly am," Jennifer grumbled, rubbing her arms. "Andy, would you please remember to help me off with my coat when we get inside? Someone may be watching."

"Don't sweat it," was Andy's response.

Polly couldn't joke around. She was just too enthralled with the night and the party and the idea of meeting the cream of New York society. The four of them would have their own room upstairs, but naturally they would have to mix with the adults, at least for a little while, just to be polite.

"Okay, guys, here goes." Cott rang the bell, and the door was immediately thrown open by a tiny, wizened old man with large, hairy ears. He was impeccably dressed in formal attire.

"Jeepers," said Andy. Jennifer poked him in the ribs, smiling sweetly.

"Hi, Monroe." Cott casually ushered them all inside.

"Good evening, sir," the butler replied with a marked accent as he tossed Cott's and Andy's coats over his arm. Then the boys helped the girls out of their coats, which they also gave to the butler. Polly tried hard not to laugh as he walked away. He looked exactly like Yoda in *The Empire Strikes Back.* "If the ladies would care to freshen up, one of the maids will escort them to the room upstairs."

Polly peered through the hallway into the living room. She couldn't believe it—it seemed just like a scene from a movie. The entire room was overflowing with flowers of every variety. Men in tuxedos and women in fabulous gowns and jewels walked around holding drinks while a pianist sat at the Steinway, playing a medley of Cole Porter tunes. Everywhere she looked, there was another celebrity—TV personalities, politicians, people from the music and dance worlds. She focused on a tall, gangly man wearing a loose-fitting, double-breasted thirties ice-cream suit and white shoes. Wasn't he a famous choreographer? This was better than a movie, of course, because she was right in the middle of it.

Seeing all the celebrities reminded Polly of the opening night party at Tavern on the Green for the musical she and Cott had attended. At that thought she felt a pang of guilt. She had never discussed the details of that night with Jennifer, and Jennifer, who had invited Andy to the ballet, had said very little about her evening. It made Polly sad that they couldn't share things the way they used to, but she was glad that Jennifer had wanted to come to the New Year's Eve party.

"Come on!" Jennifer pulled at her hand. "I want to see upstairs." She turned to Cott and Andy. "We'll be right down, okay?"

"Go ahead." Cott waved them off. "I'll go tell my dad we're here. You can all say hello, and then we'll get lost and have fun."

He led Andy into the room as the girls followed a silent young maid upstairs to one of the bedrooms that had an adjoining bathroom. She left them and closed the door soundlessly behind her.

"You mean they don't even live here all the time?" Jennifer asked, looking around the room. All the furniture was white. The thick, soft carpet was blue, and the curtains and the wallpaper were blue and white. The dust ruffle on the gigantic bed was made of the same patterned fabric as the curtains.

"Right." Polly nodded.

Jennifer walked to the other side of the room and entered the bathroom, decorated in wine-colored porcelain and chrome. The tub was on a raised white marble platform, and the mirror over the sink was lit with a halo of professional dressing-room bulbs, like the ones in theaters.

"Mr. Townsend uses this place mostly for work, but he stays over when he has late meetings or has to be in the office or fly someplace early. Cott's stepmother spent a fortune decorating this place, as you can see, but she spends most of her time in the Mamaroneck house. I haven't seen that one yet." The two girls stood in front of a full-length mirror, straightening their outfits and putting on more makeup. Jennifer hadn't been allowed to buy a new dress for the occasion, but her mother had totally torn apart and reconstructed an old dress of Nancy's. Jennifer, in a rage, had refused to even try on the dress until she saw what her mother had done with it. The sea-green chiffon that had previously hung from a conventional waistline was now a simple Grecian-style robe that fell in graceful folds over Jennifer's delicate body. The neck was low and very flattering.

Jennifer regarded herself critically. "My mom really did a good job on this, didn't she? But I wish I had the nerve to wear *that*." She pointed to Polly's clothing. "You're like an elegant harem girl or something."

Polly had discovered a wonderful Indian outfit that was so terrific on her, she had had to buy it. The top was lilac, shot through with shiny gold thread. It had full, three-quarter-length sleeves and closed down the front with a row of tiny covered buttons. The pants were voluminous and gathered at the ankle. She wore a thin headband of the same material, her mother's gold-colored flats, and a gold choker at her throat. She certainly didn't feel like dull, ordinary old Polly Luria tonight, so the rather dramatic ensemble was just right.

"I think we'd better go downstairs," she declared, checking her teeth for lipstick and starting for the door.

"After you, madame." Jennifer giggled, curtseying grandly. Together they walked down the staircase and back into the milling mob.

Cott was watching for them. He carried over two tall champagne glasses filled with cola. "These are for courage, so you can meet the folks."

"Which one is your mom?" Jennifer asked, focusing on a large, middle-aged redhead in a gold lamé sheath.

"Stepmom," he quickly corrected her. Polly gave him a look. Why did he always get so uptight about his parents? Her own parents had been divorced for years, and she hadn't seen her father since she was eight and he'd told her he was going far away for a while. He'd promised to write and give her his new address, but he never did. Sometimes that made her sad—especially on birthdays and holidays—but mostly she didn't think about it. Cott, of course, thought about his parents all the time. Maybe it was different when you had a stepmother in residence, Polly decided.

Cott glanced around. "There she is," he said, pointing. "At the piano."

Polly looked over at the young woman seated next to the pianist. She was humming along with him, sometimes breaking into the lyrics when she knew them. "That's your stepmother!" she gasped. "She's so young."

"Just—let's see. She's exactly ten years older than I am," Cott said. "Come on, I'll introduce you. By the way," he added, taking her hand, "have I told you how gorgeous you look tonight?"

"Thanks," Polly said, blushing. "You don't look so bad yourself." Cott had on a gray wool jacket with nubs of navy blue throughout the fabric. His navy slacks and maroon silk tie were the perfect accompaniments.

"Glad you like it," he whispered, elbowing his way through the crowd to get to the piano.

A line from a popular old tune wafted across the room. Cott's stepmother was accompanying the pianist. Everything about her was blond, from her platinum hair to the white clinging sheath she was wearing. Polly wondered if she'd done the living room in light wood just to match her complexion.

"Darya"—Cott cleared his throat nervously—"I'd like you to meet Polly."

"Hi!" The woman extended her hand, but she

was looking right over Polly's shoulder, as though she were wondering if there might be somebody more interesting on the horizon.

"Oh, darling," she breathed in a husky voice, touching Cott lightly on the arm. "I really need to see Mitch, you know what I mean? I just can't handle all these people. Some crush, huh?" she suddenly turned to Jennifer for her opinion.

But before she could respond, Mitch Townsend was at his wife's side. "Wow," Darya said in a breathy tone, "you must have felt the vibes, sweetie. Like you know I wanted to see you."

Polly stood there, feeling very awkward. No wonder Cott had so much trouble around these people. How could you ever figure out the right thing to say to them? With her mother and the Taruskins, she felt like she belonged—like they all spoke the same language. She glanced at Cott and saw that I-don't-care look on his face. *That must be his way of coping,* she decided. *That's why he tries to act so cool and sophisticated sometimes.*

"Well, good evening," Mitch Townsend said in a hearty tone.

"Mitch, this is Jennifer Taruskin and Andy Donahue; they go to Mamaroneck High, too. And you've met Polly."

"Have a great time, all of you." Mitch shook Andy's hand hastily and glanced at Jennifer before turning to Polly. "And how are you tonight?" he asked her. When he looked at her,

113

his face suddenly got very intense, and he studied her features as though he were reading a map.

"Fine, thanks, Mr. Townsend. Um, happy New Year." Polly was desperately hoping that Cott could rescue them from all this and whisk them upstairs.

"Can't say that yet, Polly. It's only ten-thirty." He turned to his wife. "Come over here, dear," he said, helping her up from the piano bench. "The senator needs another drink."

The Townsends wandered to the opposite side of the room, and Polly breathed a sigh of relief. "Let's start *our* party," she whispered to Cott, taking him by the arm, but Cott was very preoccupied. She followed his gaze across the room to his father, who was talking to the thin, gangly young man Polly thought she'd recognized when she walked in. Mr. Townsend was pointing right at them.

"What's going on?" she asked.

"Beats me. Mitch is up to something, though." He frowned. "That man would find a way to make a business deal on a desert island." Then he pushed her in the direction of the staircase. "Your ballroom awaits," he said in a gallant manner. "Upstairs."

The four of them charged the steps, and Cott led them to the top floor of the townhouse. There was a comfortable den and a beautiful glass-covered conservatory filled with incredible tropical flowers and plants. Beyond these two rooms was another large living room. The furniture had all been cleared to the sides.

Cott walked in and gestured to the heavily laden table next to the stereo. "Fortification," he explained. There was an abundant array of cold cuts, pâtés and cheeses, as well as bottles of orange juice, Coke, and 7-Up. He slipped a cassette into the tape deck, and Willie Nelson's voice singing "Moonlight in Vermont" filled the large room.

"Dance?" Cott asked Polly. She nodded happily and put her hand on his shoulder. He drew her close and moved her slowly around the floor. Polly let the music fill her mind and heart, and she closed her eyes, enjoying the mellow sounds and feelings inside her. As she breathed in the scent of Cott's after-shave and felt the rough, shaved skin of his chin against her forehead and let her small hand relax inside his large one, she understood why it was so nice to have a boyfriend. It was nothing like having a best friend, who was almost a mirror image; a boyfriend was separate in so many ways and yet closer than a girlfriend could ever be.

The sweet song ended, and the bouncy rhythm of "On the Sunny Side of the Street" took its place. Polly was shaken out of her reverie by the sound of Jennifer's voice. "Oh, this is heaven!" Cott and Polly went over to the table, where Andy had already made himself a huge sandwich out of every item on the buffet and Jennifer was spooning pearls of black caviar out of a glass bowl.

"Cott, you're a sweetie! You promised me fish eggs, and here they are!"

He shrugged. "Hate the stuff myself. What do you think, Polly?"

Polly looked dubiously at the little black dots swimming in their own inky juice. "I don't think—" She wrinkled her nose.

"Oh, taste!" Jennifer was clearly delighted with the new delicacy. She held out her spoon to Polly, who sucked a few pearls into her mouth. She bit down, and the caviar exploded gently on her tongue. "Hmm," she deliberated. "Pretty fishy, if you ask me."

Cott poured Polly a Coke and began arranging a variety of foods on a plate for her. "Eat up," he encouraged her as she popped a black olive into her mouth. "Wait'll you see the dessert!"

They were enjoying their meal and listening to Fleetwood Mac, when there was a knock at the door. They looked over to see Mitch Townsend holding a glass of champagne.

"Sorry to intrude," he said hastily, walking toward them.

"Oh, no," Cott muttered under his breath. Polly squeezed his hand.

"It's sort of noisy down there"—he pointed in the direction of the main party—"so I thought I'd see what was doing up here." Staring straight at Polly, he added, "Cott, would you turn that thing down a little?"

Cott sighed and went to adjust the sound level on the stereo.

"So, Polly," Mitch said, taking a seat on the side of the buffet table, "Cott tells me you're a dancer."

"We both are," Polly nodded, gesturing to Jennifer.

"I see." He smoothed his mustache. "What kind of dance? How long have you studied?"

"Mostly ballet. For as long as we can remember," Jennifer cut in. Polly wondered why he was so interested. This wasn't exactly the sort of thing you discussed at a New Year's Eve party with your son's date.

"Polly, listen," he said, getting up and starting to pace the long room. "I've just been talking about you with one of my guests downstairs. Do you know Bill Thompson, the choreographer?"

"Of course. Who doesn't?" Polly shook her head. So *that's* who he was. Thompson, who'd imprinted his signature on modern dance by combining ballet with interpretive, dramatic, jazzy stuff. He was the hottest thing on Broadway.

"Yes, well, he and I are working on a special for Shirley MacLaine next month. It's going to be kind of a one-woman show, see. She'll dance a lot, sing a few songs—"

Cott slipped a Stones tape into the machine and "Jumpin' Jack Flash" began to drown out his father. Polly knew he just hated what was happening, so he was being rude on purpose.

"Cott, will you do me the favor of turning that thing off for a minute?" Townsend asked sharply. Jennifer gave Polly a look. Cott did as he was told, and suddenly the room seemed very quiet.

"Now," Mitch said, turning back to Polly, "the reason I'm telling you all this is that Thompson and I are thinking of putting a dream sequence into the show. It'll be Shirley as a teenager, see, to give the idea of her beginnings—how she got started as a young dancer. So Bill and I, we were just looking at your features and height. The coloring is wrong, but we can fix that with a wig and makeup. You're a good type. It could work."

Polly just stared at him. "You mean, you want me—?"

"We can audition you Tuesday, see how you look on camera, how you move, how you take direction, how you read. It's going to be a very crucial spot. The girl who does it has to carry the whole five-minute segment alone. So, are you interested?"

"I—uh—" Polly was too dumbfounded to get out a coherent response. She was very grateful when Cott jumped in for her.

"Mitch, why don't you let her sleep on it, and

118

she'll call you in the morning. This is New Year's Eve, you know," he added pointedly.

"Yeah, right. Good idea, kid. Here, Polly." He withdrew a leather card case from the inside pocket of his tux and produced a simple card engraved with his name and phone number. "Give me a ring, say, by four tomorrow. It'll be a terrific spot, believe me," he assured her on his way out the door.

Cott immediately let the Stones wail again.

"Oh, my God!" said Polly.

"Are you really going to do this?" Jennifer got up and came over to her.

"Well, I have to audition. I couldn't turn it down."

"Hey, I think it's great, Polly," Andy chimed in. "You could be an overnight star."

"Or she could just ruin her whole career," Jennifer said, cutting him off.

Polly sighed and turned away from her friend. She certainly wasn't in the mood for one of Jennifer's grouchy warnings right now. Everything was too magical tonight.

"I'm serious, Polly. If Balanchine ever found out that you'd done commercial stuff, he'd write you off."

"I don't agree," Polly said staunchly. "He'd probably be impressed that I had a real professional credential."

"Oh, sure," Jennifer said. "As Shirley MacLaine's double?"

"Why don't you two shut up for a second," Cott suggested, taking Polly into his arms. "This is a party, okay. We're supposed to be celebrating."

"What do you think?" Polly asked Cott when Jennifer had been dragged aside by Andy and coerced into a slow dance.

Cott shrugged. "Can't hurt you." He looked as if he didn't want to talk about it.

"Well, will you come with me?" she asked impetuously. "I couldn't go in all alone for this audition."

He smiled and twirled her under his arm. "You're on. And now can we please just forget it?"

"I'll try." They danced on until they were hot and sweaty, stopping only occasionally for a sip of Coke or a nibble of cheese. Polly tried to lose herself in the dancing, and when the slow numbers came on, she let Cott lead her gently around as she clung to him and allowed her mind to wander.

Suddenly Andy looked at his watch. "Hey, we're going to miss it!"

Cott took Polly by the hand, and the four of them raced down the two flights of stairs. A group of very silly grownups was sitting around on the floor of the den, watching the Zenith large-screen projection TV. The ball was all lit up, sitting on top of the Allied Chemical Building.

"I love New Year's," one elderly woman encased

in yards of pearls exclaimed, "because I can start my life all over again the next day. A brand new beginning."

Polly smiled up at Cott, and he squeezed her hand. As she looked across at Jennifer, she was glad to see that she and Andy had their arms around each other and were gazing into each other's eyes.

A brand new beginning, she thought, taking a deep breath. *Maybe it will be. Maybe I can have it all—a boyfriend, a best friend, and even a shot at my very own TV spot.*

Just then, the white ball dropped, and the sound of bells, whistles, and cheers filled the house and the street outside.

"Happy New Year!" everyone screamed. Someone threw a streamer on Polly's head.

"I hope it's a very happy one," Cott whispered. He was so close she could feel his warmth breath on her cheek. His soft words cut right through everything, despite the noise and confusion around them. He leaned down, and his lips naturally, easily, slid down her cheek to her mouth. She thrilled to the sensation of him holding her tightly but delicately, as though she were too precious to lose. The noise was now deafening.

"Happy New Year," she mouthed when he let her go. They clutched each other's hands, and both of them were smiling. "It's the best one I've ever had."

"Me, too," Cott agreed.

When Jimmy drove them all home to Mamaroneck in the limousine at two in the morning, Polly rested her head on Cott's shoulder, let the motion of the car lull her into a drowsy stupor, and thought about the evening. She felt as if her whole life had suddenly changed. She looked to her right and saw that Jennifer and Andy were dozing together on the end of the seat. She had thought Cott was asleep, too, but when she looked into his face, she saw that his eyes were open.

"I like you so much, Polly," he said quietly.

She couldn't speak; her heart was too full. All she could do was kiss him softly and snuggle closer to him for the long ride home.

Chapter Eight

New Year's morning was cold and clear. Jennifer hadn't slept a wink. After the limousine had dropped her at home, she'd gone into the kitchen for some milk. And she began to think. So much was happening so fast, and she wasn't sure about any of it. When she finally went to bed about four, she was exhausted but very determined.

She waited until ten to go over and ring the Luria's bell. No one was up at the Taruskins' when Jennifer bundled up in two sweaters, hat, scarf, boots, and her down jacket to brave the January cold. The frozen streets would obviously make bicycling impossible, so she just steeled herself against the elements and set out on foot.

She rang the Luria's bell twice before Polly answered, yawning and shivering in her blue terry-cloth robe. "What are you doing here? What time is it?" she hissed, rubbing her scalp and hopping from one bare foot to the other.

"Can I come in? I want to talk."

"Oh, boy," Polly grumbled, pulling her friend into the warm kitchen. "You do pick the best times for sincerity." She put some water on the stove to boil. While she measured out the coffee into a filter, she asked over her shoulder, "Have a good time last night? Or should I say this morning?" Then she looked at the clock. "For Pete's sake, Jen, we hardly got to sleep."

"I know. Yeah, it was a good party." She pulled off her hat and rubbed her stiff fingers together.

"You seemed to be having more fun with Andy than you used to."

"Well, I have to admit you were right. I just never appreciated him. Maybe he grew on me. Or I grew into him. Polly," Jennifer blurted out, "are you going to do this thing? Audition for him?"

Polly turned off the whistling kettle and poured the boiling water into the coffee. "I don't see why not."

"You don't? Then listen to me, because I do. In the first place, Madame will kill you when she finds out. You know what she thinks about anything that isn't strictly classical. In the second place, what about all the *real* dancing you have to do before this summer? I mean, we've discussed this for years, Polly. There are serious dancers, and then there are those who get by on personality and a couple of high kicks. That's such bull! You can't throw away your real career. And in the third—"

"Oh, Jennifer." Polly eased herself into the kitchen chair opposite her friend and sat on her feet. "I wish you wouldn't give me a lecture right now. Just think of it this way: if *you* had a chance like this, would you pass it up? And it's only an audition, right? I probably won't even make it."

Jennifer sighed and took off her jacket and one sweater. "That's not the point."

"What *is* the point?" Polly demanded angrily, getting up to pour them two cups of coffee. She nearly spilled it because her hand was shaking. "You've been picking at me for one thing or another ever since October, and it seems to me this is just something new to criticize."

Jennifer looked like she was going to cry. "Why are you so different, Polly? You never used to be this way. But ever since you started going out with him—" She couldn't continue, and she took a gulp of the scalding coffee, hoping that her burned tongue would hurt more than the pain inside.

Polly wanted to do something to make it all right again, but it was too late. They had grown too far apart in just a few short months. All she could do was say, "I'm sorry. Really I am." She couldn't bear to feel so lost and alone. Even thinking about Cott didn't help.

"It's just—" she went on, "I mean, I really care about Cott, but that has nothing to do with you and me. We'll always be best friends—at least *I* want us to be. I know we haven't spent lots of time together or shared stuff like we used to, but, well, maybe that's good for us," she finished lamely.

"Not for me!" Jennifer exploded, unable to hold in her sobs any longer. "I can see wanting to go out with him. He's so rich and everything, so you have all these exciting parties to go to and celebrities to meet. That's hard to say no to. I know I couldn't. But he doesn't care about your dance career. Don't you remember our plan, Polly? We were going to—"

"Meet two wonderful guys and go out with them all through college and buy houses next to one another and have great careers in dance, too."

Jennifer was astounded that Polly had actually remembered the whole thing. "I guess life doesn't always work out so neat and clean, huh?" she said, sniffling.

"Guess not." They sat silently for a minute, staring into their cups. When the kitchen door swung open and Jane Luria walked in, neither of them even looked up.

"Well," she said, yawning, "obviously you girls don't think this is a *happy* New Year's."

"Sorry, Mom," Polly said, getting up to go over and kiss her on the cheek. "We're just tired from last night."

"You're not the only one," Mrs. Luria agreed. "How was your fancy party?"

"Oh, great," Jennifer said very solemnly. "We even had caviar."

"Really?" Mrs. Luria's eyelids suddenly pried themselves apart. "Boy, that's better than what I got. Quiche, quiche, and more quiche at Sally Lipset's. Who was attending this elegant soiree?"

"Oh, lots of famous types," Polly said casually. "Even Bill Thompson, the choreographer." Jennifer gave her a look, but Polly was bursting to tell. "Mom, they want me to dance for them. For a TV special."

"Aren't you girls a little old for the Sugarplum Fairies?" She laughed.

"No, Mrs. Luria. They want Polly," Jennifer said. "It's not ballet, either."

"It's a solo, Mom," Polly cut in, her eyes shining. "A dream sequence where I get to be a young Shirley MacLaine. And Thompson's going to choreograph a segment for me!"

Her mother nodded in her typical accepting manner. "Well, so long childhood. Hello the life of a working stiff. Polly, are you ready for this? Answer me truthfully."

Jennifer's eyes were glistening again. She wanted Polly to say no. But she realized everything that was at stake for her best friend. And when she asked herself what she would do in Polly's situation, she simply couldn't ignore the fact that the offer was very, very tempting. There were no easy answers.

"I really think I *am* ready," Polly said slowly. "And even if I'm not, it would be stupid not to give it my best shot, right?"

Mrs. Luria looked at Jennifer and shrugged. "Guess there's no arguing with her."

"Huh-uh." Jennifer was determined not to cry again. She told herself over and over that it wasn't up to her to judge Polly's decision. She tried very hard to say the words, "I wish you lots of luck, and I hope you make it," but somehow, she couldn't quite bring herself to be *that* big about it.

Polly looked at the kitchen clock and then at her best friend. "I have to call Mr. Townsend at four with my answer. Please stick around."

"Sure," Jennifer said bravely.

"Want to go for a walk?"

"Okay. Where to?"

"How about the drugstore on East Prospect? There was a sign up yesterday saying they'd be open."

Mrs. Luria got up. "I need a nap after all this excitment. If you two insist on freezing your tootsies off, that's your business." Just before she walked out of the kitchen, she turned and smiled softly at her daughter. "I'll be up by four, though, hon, in case you need me for anything."

Polly ran upstairs quickly to throw on some clothes, and then she joined Jennifer back in the kitchen. "Ready?"

She opened the door, and they were hit with a blast of cold wind. "Ugh, why are we doing this?" Jennifer grumbled.

"It's invigorating," Polly assured her. "Besides, I have to get something."

"What?" Jennifer squeezed her eyes shut against the cold air and rearranged her muffler so it would cover her mouth.

"Suntan lotion," Polly stated, walking along beside her friend, pushing back against the fierce wind.

"Very funny."

"No, I need it. It's a good-luck charm," she explained.

They passed rows of neat houses, some of them with plumes of smoke wafting out of the chimneys. No one was on the streets; it was like having Mamaroneck all to themselves for the New Year.

"I don't get it," Jennifer mumbled through the wool scarf.

"Well, Mr. Townsend comes from California. Nice sunny climate. Hot and tropical. So," she concluded, "suntan lotion!"

"I don't get it," Jennifer repeated. The logic of

all this escaped her. She wanted to give Polly another lecture about her commitment to ballet, but it was too hard to talk while walking into the wind.

Polly laughed and walked a little more quickly. "Don't question everything, Jennifer. Sometimes you just have to go with the flow." They had reached the little row of shops on Mamaroneck Avenue, all closed for the holidays except for the drugstore around the corner on East Prospect, where a small girl was just pulling the front door shut with great difficulty.

They walked inside, glad to be warm at last. Polly went directly to the shelves and scanned them for the product of her choice. In a second she spotted the bottle she wanted. Jennifer was at the front counter examining eye shadow sticks.

"I can't miss now," Polly smiled, triumphantly holding up the Coppertone, but she couldn't get Jennifer to smile back. As she reached into her back pocket with one hand for the five-dollar bill she had put there, she grabbed Jennifer's arm with the other. "I promise I won't be a different person, Jen. I promise I'll always be there for you. I'm scared of this, too, you know."

"I know." Jennifer nodded gravely and reached over to squeeze Polly's hand. They paid for the lotion and then walked back to Polly's house, not talking very much.

                        *   *   *

At ten of four, Mrs. Luria, Polly, and Jennifer
were sitting around the kitchen table, staring
at Mr. Townsend's card. Now that she'd had a
chance to think about it, Mrs. Luria seemed
more apprehensive about the audition than she
had that morning.

"Remember to ask about joining the union
and having a contract," she cautioned Polly.
"And billing! That's important. You should be
high up in the credits in big print!"

Polly laughed, exchanging an amused look
with Jennifer. "Mom, where'd you learn all this
stuff?"

Mrs. Luria exhaled sharply. "You can't forget
my one summer of summer stock!" She looked
shocked at Polly's lapse in memory.

"Oh, yeah," Polly recalled. "Before she married my dad," Polly explained to Jennifer, "she
gave the theater a whirl. *That* lasted a long
time."

"Yes, and I gave it all up for real estate," Mrs.
Luria said, giving a mock sigh. Jennifer burst
out laughing. "Okay, okay, so are you going to
call or aren't you?"

"I'm calling," Polly declared, lifting the phone
from the receiver. This could just be the most
important phone call she'd ever make, she
thought, concentrating on the bottle of Copper-

tone perched on the table. It gave her a little courage, but not much.

A sleepy-sounding voice answered at the New York apartment. "Ah, Mrs. Townsend, I hope I didn't wake you," Polly said nervously. "This is Cott's friend, Polly Luria."

"Oh, wow, sure," was the woman's lethargic response. "Just hold on, okay?" Then she said, "I think he isn't here."

"Ah, I know that, Mrs. Townsend. He took me home last night. Actually, I wanted to speak with Mr. Townsend. He told me to call him today. About a part in a TV show." Then in a horrified flash of forgotten manners, Polly blurted out, "And the party was fantastic, Mrs. Townsend. Jennifer and Andy loved it, too."

Jennifer rolled her eyes at Polly across the kitchen table. Jane Luria made a hurry-up motion with her hands.

"Um. Could I speak to your husband, please?" Polly added.

"Oh, sure. Mitch!" Darya sang out on the other end of the line.

And in an instant, Mitchell Townsend was saying hello to Polly. Her heart flew to her throat.

"And how are you this morning?" he asked in a jovial tone.

It was afternoon. Didn't he know that? Or was it a joke? But she couldn't correct him. "Oh, fine, great, as a matter of fact," Polly said heartily. "How are you?"

"Pretty good for the day after New Year's Eve," he said. Then he cleared his throat purposefully. "Now, what about my offer?"

"Well," Polly said slowly, licking her lips and crossing her fingers, "I'd really love to audition for you. It sounds like a wonderful opportunity."

"Good. Glad you think so."

Polly heard the sound of a pencil tapping on a surface, and she gave him a second to write a note to himself or whatever he was doing. "Ah, could you tell me something more about this?" Polly tried to ignore her mother, who was mouthing a lot of insistent questions about contracts, unions, and billing.

"Sure," Townsend said. "You come on in Tuesday morning say eleven, Studio H on the fourth floor of 30 Rockefeller Plaza. Bill Thompson'll give you a few routines, and we'll do a little screen test. Then we'll play you back on the videotape and see what we've got. If we like you and the deal sounds workable, you get the part. If you do well in the part, we talk about that movie."

"Movie!" Polly squeaked. Surely she hadn't heard right.

"Movie?" Jennifer asked, a puzzled look on her face. Mrs. Luria was now gesturing wildly.

"Didn't I mention it to you last night?" Mitchell Townsend was vaguely apologetic, as though he felt he hadn't completed the offer in a truly businesslike manner.

"Well, no, I don't really remember."

"Yeah, okay. Thompson and I were talking about considering the same girl we use for this show in a feature film he's currently working on in Hollywood. Kind of artsy—there are some dancing roles in it. So who knows? It's a possibility anyway. Keep your options open."

Polly couldn't believe he was talking about hiring her for both a TV show and a movie as if he were going to the corner to buy a quart of milk. Except that Mitchell Townsend had probably never bought a quart of milk by himself in his entire life.

"It certainly sounds like something I should consider." She thought she was going to pass out if she didn't get to the end of the phone conversation soon. "Hollywood as well as this special."

"Hollywood!" her mother and Jennifer screamed at exactly the same moment. Polly wanted to die of shame. He must have heard them all the way over on Sutton Place.

"Good," he told her as she waved frantically at the two crazed women beside her, trying to shut them up. "Then we'll see you Tuesday. Bring your regular dance class stuff, toe shoes, too. And happy New Year, Polly," he added, chuckling.

"Oh, the same to *you*, Mr. Townsend," Polly breathed. "A very happy one." *Wait'll I tell Cott,* she kept thinking.

"Take care. Ciao."

"Bye." She hung up and stared at the bottle of Coppertone on the table. Mrs. Luria was jumping around wildly. Jennifer just sat at the table, shaking her head thoughtfully.

"Tell me! What did he say?" Jane Luria insisted.

"Polly, what are you getting yourself into now?" Jennifer, after her brief explosion, had settled back into her cynical attitude about the whole thing.

"He said that if I get the part and they like me, there's a chance at a movie role in a Hollywood dance film. At least I think that's what he said." Polly knocked one hand against the side of her head. She had to be dreaming. She was going to wake up any minute.

"Well, if you ask me—" Jennifer began, her hands on her hips.

There was a knock on the kitchen door, and Mrs. Luria flew to open it. It was Cott. "Hi everyone!" he said as Mrs. Luria ushered him in. Then, practically skipping out of the kitchen, she blew a kiss at the three of them and left the room. "I tried to call, but it was busy," he said as he shrugged off his coat and draped it over a chair.

"I was just talking to your dad, that's why." Polly smiled, got up, and went over to hug him.

"Oh, yeah?" He reached over to swipe a cook-

135

ing from the plate lying on the kitchen counter beside the stove. "How's dear old dad this afternoon?"

"Just fine." Polly could not wipe the grin off her face. There was so much to tell, so much happening at once.

"Well, this is where I came in," Jennifer muttered, picking up her things and starting for the door. "No," she added when Polly seemed to be about to ask her to stay. "Honest. I really did promise to be home by five. Hey, Pol," she said, forcing a smile, "I'm really happy for you." And then she was gone, leaving Cott and Polly alone in the kitchen.

"I take it you're going to dance for him," Cott said after the door had closed behind Jennifer.

Polly nodded. "I feel dizzy." She giggled. "I better sit down."

Cott took a seat across from her and took her hands in his. "It couldn't happen to a nicer girl," he said softly. And when she blushed and shook her head, he added, "No, I mean that." Then he started laughing uproariously.

"What's so funny?"

"You are something else," he stated, picking up the bottle on the table. "Who else do I know who'd use Coppertone on New Year's Day in Mamaroneck when it's five degrees outside?"

"But can't you see?" she asked, pointing at her head. "I've got sunstroke."

"I don't know about that," he responded quietly, stroking the top of her hand with one finger. "But you sure are glowing all over." He leaned closer and kissed her gently on her forehead.

Polly decided then and there that this was probably what heaven was all about.

Chapter Nine

The elevator door slid open on the fourth floor. The girls stepped out and hesitantly began walking toward the sign that read Studios A–H.

"Where is he?" Polly hissed to Jennifer. She was so nervous that she was clutching her knapsack in a death grip.

"Be cool. He's never let you down yet, right?" Jennifer took charge of the situation, walking down the corridor briskly toward a security guard, who was seated at a small table reading the paper. "Excuse me," she said, "can you tell us which is H?"

The man pointed without a word or a smile. Jennifer steered Polly in the correct direction. She knew from the glazed look in her friend's eyes that Polly was not all there.

"He said to go right in and they'll take you to the dressing room. You brought everything?"

"I guess," Polly said absently. She was praying

that Cott would appear out of nowhere and take her away from all this. But at the same time, she realized it was far too late for escape.

"Come on in," said a deep, hearty voice. The door to Studio H was propped open, and a small balding man stood before them holding a clipboard.

"You Polly?" he asked Polly.

She gulped and nodded.

"I'm Sam, production manager. They're all waiting for you." He jerked a thumb toward another door. It had a big sign on it that read: It is expressly forbidden to open this door when the red light is on!

Jennifer gave Polly a push, and they walked into the control booth where Cott was sitting with his father, Bill Thompson, and three other men.

Polly nearly sobbed with relief. "Cott—"

He came to her at once and pulled her to one side of the room. "Hi, babe. How're you feelin'?"

"Sick. Really, I mean it's bad."

"You'll be okay once you start moving."

"I don't think I can lift one toe." Polly bit her lip. "This is much worse than the scholarship audition."

"Listen," Cott said, pulling her close in a big bear hug, "I won't let 'em eat you."

"Hey!" Polly said, suddenly snapping out o' her preoccupied trance. "Are those new glasses?"

"Yup," Cott smiled, touching the thin, gray

frames. "I got these for you. Clear lenses, so you can see what I'm thinking."

"That's nice," she said, grinning.

"Polly?" A painfully thin, beautifully dressed young woman interrupted them. "Would you come with me, please? I'll take you to the dressing room."

Jennifer gave Polly a sympathetic look as she was marched away, and then she went to sit next to Cott. "Poor kid. She looks like she's going to a hanging." Jennifer was terribly concerned. She knew how Polly sometimes made mistakes when she was nervous. Although she had been against the whole idea of this TV special at first, Jennifer had come around in the past two days, having decided that if Polly ever needed her best friend, it was now. She would stand by her through all of this.

"Polly's a trouper," Cott murmured. "She'll be okay."

By the time he had pointed out the director, the lighting designer, and the chief cameraman to Jennifer, Polly was ready. Bill Thompson got up and left the control room, wandering languidly out into the huge studio to start the audition.

Polly had dressed very carefully. She wore her pink tights and toe shoes with a long-sleeved, wraparound forest green leotard and matching short rehearsal skirt. For years, Mme Mishkin had been drilling into her the necessity of mak-

141

ing an immediate physical impression on an audience. "Eef you forget the steps, pah, they will pass queekly. But eef the pipple forget *you*, this is the end. *Kaput*." Polly knew the green leotard contrasted well with her dark hair and the flow of the rehearsal skirt's fabric would show how well she moved.

"Hi, Pol. I'm Bill Thompson." He extended his hand to her, and she clasped it, hoping he would ignore her cold, clammy fingers. He seemed very much at ease, a towel around his long neck, a tight red T-shirt and black draw-string pants covering his elongated frame. "Okay, are you ready? I assume you've already warmed up."

Polly froze. Why hadn't anyone told her? "Ah—I'm all set," she answered nervously.

Thompson took her by the hand and led her to the center of the studio. She nearly tripped over a huge cable and then was almost blinded by the wide-angled lights hanging at all levels over her head.

Thompson smiled at her confusion. "You just watch me and just think about dancing. These guys"—he waved impatiently at the three cam-eramen hiding behind their large machines— "are just along for the ride. It's *our* show."

Despite his reassurance, Polly was practically paralyzed with anxiety. She'd never been in a situation like this and was afraid she'd forget everything as soon as Thompson asked her to do something.

"Okay," he said, extending his arms to either side. "Let's start with a simple combination—I'm sure you've done this before. And . . . step, close, step, walk, walk. Turn, kick, cross, and together. Drop and push off, drop and knee turn, rock back on your heels and finish. And then repeat to the opposite side. Got that?" He turned and smiled at her.

Oh, God, what did he do? Polly drew a complete blank. "Ah, could you just go over that once more?"

Thompson exhaled sharply. "Polly, you've got to watch me. This isn't kindergarten, you know. You're up for a job."

"Yes, okay." She nodded nervously. "I'm just a little—it's just the lights and wires, see. I'll get it this time," she added adamantly.

He shrugged and went through the routine again, this time throwing in some fancy details with his arms and head. He also moved his hips as if they were disconnected from the rest of him. Polly marked the steps for herself as he moved and then attempted her own version of it, concentrating on doing everything just right.

"Great, terrific. Again!" Thompson ordered, waving to the control booth. "Okay, Pol, now loosen up. Give me the feel of it, not the individual steps."

What does he mean by that? Polly mused,

throwing her head back the way she'd seen him do it. In ballet the precision of the steps was the most important thing.

Just when she was on the verge of giving up, he stopped and decided to give her a chance to do something that would show her off to best advantage. "You have a prepared piece?" he asked.

"Oh, yes!" she exclaimed. "My friend has the tape in there." She gestured wildly to Jennifer in the control booth, who immediately produced a cassette from her purse and handed it to the director. It was the segment from *Giselle* that Polly had used for her scholarship audition.

Thompson wiped his face with his towel and moved aside. "Go ahead. Just be careful to watch these white lines on the floor. Don't go outside them. And one other thing. You've got three cameras on you, see, and I want you to be aware of which one has the red light on. They'll switch back and forth, focusing on you. Your job is to play to the lit red light, okay?"

He walked back through the door to the control room, and Polly was alone with the cameras. She heard the musical introduction filter through the powerful speakers, and she breathed deeply, trying to get herself into the mood. As the flutes and oboes died away, she raised herself on her toes and began to move.

Don't think about the red lights. Don't think about the marks. Just perform like crazy! Then, in the back of her head, she heard Mme Mishkin's loud, firm voice. *Plees, mademoiselle! You look now as eef you are in great pain. Will you smile, plees?*

Polly grinned at the red eye following her and went into her routine. She didn't count, she didn't even think. She just danced.

"She's perfect. I love her," Mitch Townsend kept repeating over and over.

"She seems to have trouble taking direction, Mitch," Thompson reminded him, not taking his eyes off Polly. Every monitor in the control room had another image of Polly's arabesque now. There were dozens of Pollys along the back wall, all poised gracefully on one foot.

"She picked it up, didn't she?" Mitch said impatiently, writing copious notes in his small black book. "Get Sam in here for the reading. Jim, what do you think?"

The young director kept watching Polly. "I like her. Nice quality. Very fresh."

Cott and Jennifer grinned at one another.

Mitch spoke into the intercom. "Polly," would you stay right there a sec?" Then he turned to Cott and waved an annoyed hand at him. "You two get lost. We have to talk."

Cott led Jennifer into the hallway. She began biting her nails. On the one hand, she wanted Polly to get this because she was a great dancer and she deserved the part and she was her best friend. On the other hand, wouldn't it drive them further apart? She wasn't sure.

Cott leaned against the faded gray-green wall. He had a little smile on his face. "Don't sweat it, Jen," he said. "I've seen my father in action more times than I can count. I know how he thinks and what he likes."

The thin woman who had taken Polly to the dressing room walked past them. "You two can go in if you want."

Sam, the production manager who had greeted the girls at the door, strolled into the studio carrying two scripts.

"Polly," Jim, the director said into the mike as Cott and Jennifer took their seats again, "we have just one more thing for you to do and then you can go home, okay?"

Go home, Polly thought in a panic. *That means I blew it, right?*

Sam handed her one of the scripts, and she had to tell her fingers to close over the pages.

"Ever do any acting, Polly?" the director questioned.

"Um. Not exactly. Dance is more my thing." *Oh God, now they want me to be Meryl Streep!* She kept licking her lips, but her mouth was so dry she couldn't get them wet.

"Okay, Sam, pick it up from the middle of page six. Polly, this is the scene between the young girl and the director who first lets her into his studio at night so she can rehearse

146

alone. Barry Newton will be playing this part in the special, but Sam will read it with you now."

Barry Newton! She couldn't count how many nights she and Jennifer had watched his private-eye series on T.V. He was a wonderfully craggy-looking actor with wavy brown hair and ice blue eyes, and he had a crooked, sexy smile that was just devastating to Polly. If she ever had to say hello, let alone read a scene with him, she'd just die!

" 'You new around here?' " Sam read to her in a bored monotone from the script. He sounded as if he were reading a grocery list.

Polly stared at the lines of dialogue on the page and cleared her throat. She didn't know how to act, so she'd just try to be natural and speak as though she were talking to somebody. " 'I hope—' " She stopped in dismay. It sounded more like a bleat than a word.

She took her time and tried to pretend she knew what she was doing. Of course, she hadn't the faintest idea. " 'I hope you don't mind,' " she read shyly to a yawning Sam. At least she'd managed to get control of her voice. " 'I saw the door open, and I just came in to look around. I'll leave if you want me to.' "

" 'Naw, that's okay, kid. Dance your brains out.' "

And then it was over. Polly was breathless when Mitch called over the intercom, "Come on in here, Polly." The people in the booth were all conferring and looked very preoccupied as Sam led her through the connecting door. No one except Cott and Jennifer was paying attention to her. *Well, that's it,* Polly thought resignedly. *At least I can say I tried.*

"Polly, have a seat," Thompson said.

Polly was only aware of Cott taking her by the hand and seating her next to his father. Then she heard the words, "We really like you, Polly. You'll be fine."

"You mean—" she began, trying to grasp the situation.

"You got the part, silly," Jennifer whispered on her other side. "Congratulations!"

Cott wrapped an arm around her shoulders and kissed her on the cheek. Mr. Townsend was dictating notes to the thin woman, and she was writing everything down on her clipboard. Sam pressed a form into her hand and told her to fill it out. Bill Thompson said something about her nice elevation, but she didn't really hear.

Polly, you're hired! You're going to be on TV! Wake up! yelled a little voice inside her. All she could think of was that her mouth was so dry she couldn't even swallow.

". . . and we'll get the forms by tomorrow for your union card—we pay the dues. I guess you don't have an agent, right?" Mitch Townsend's question penetrated her fog.

"No, she doesn't," Jennifer answered promptly.

"Well, I'll give her mother a call this evening then, and we'll talk salary."

"And billing," Jennifer cut in. Mitch Townsend threw back his head and roared. "What do you mean she doesn't have an agent?"

Polly felt consciousness returning at last, and she reached over with her free hand, the one Cott wasn't squeezing to death, to shake Mr. Townsend's.

"I promise I'll do a great job. Really. Thanks so much! And you, too, Mr. Thompson," she added hastily.

"See you at nine sharp tomorrow morning," Thompson said. "We have lots of work to do."

Polly, Cott, and Jennifer were ushered out of the booth, and after Polly had changed quickly back into her street clothes, they went downstairs together in the elevator. "I can't believe it," Polly kept muttering, turning from one friend to the other, a look of amazement on her face.

"You deserved it," Cott said easily.

"That was a pretty neat trick, following all those weird things Thompson was giving you," Jennifer concurred. "It's sure to throw all your training off, but, well, so what?"

"So what? Jennifer, are you feeling okay?" Polly asked, reaching over to put a hand on her friend's forehead. "No lecture? No warning? No nothing?"

Jennifer sighed as they stepped out of the elevator. "I guess I was kind of pressing my own

149

ideas on you. We may be close, but we're not the same person. So I have to admit it; there *are* some things other than a life in ballet."

"No," Polly said in total disbelief, shaking her head.

"No? Well, not for me, of course, but possibly for you." Jennifer smiled. "That is until you snap back into your right mind."

"There," Polly told Cott triumphantly, throwing up her hands. "I know nothing had changed." The three of them erupted in simultaneous laughter.

"Promenade Cafe!" Cott insisted. "My treat." He raced them past the holiday tourists through the long hallways of Rockefeller Center.

The cafe was still filled with a lunchtime crowd, but after a short wait, they got a table with a view of the skating rink. The professionals were doing their turns and leaps in the center, while toddlers and teenagers skated slowly along the edges, falling down and picking themselves up again. There was one couple who must have been in their sixties, dancing together on the ice like two kids.

They ordered, and then the girls rushed to the phone booths to call home with the extraordinary news. Polly got back to the table first.

"Hello, pretty lady." Cott smiled at her beaming face. "You look like you're feeling okay."

"I am." Polly sat beside him and gazed out at

the skaters. "I could swoop and glide and spin without stopping for a month."

"Now, can I get you alone for a date sometime? Before you fly off to California?"

Polly looked into his face. Suddenly he seemed very somber. "Of course," she answered earnestly.

"It's just, well, every time I run into something fabulous, I lose it."

Polly was shocked to hear him talk this way. She hadn't even realized how deeply he felt or that he was just as nervous about her success as Jennifer was. Funny, all the time she'd been so guilty about neglecting her best friend, and now she saw that she had done much the same thing to Cott. He was left out because she was doing something that didn't include him. But it did include his father, and that made it even worse.

"I won't ever leave you, Cott," she said fiercely. "You can count on that."

He breathed a sigh of relief and then turned back to the window to watch the elderly couple dance gracefully and intimately together on the ice.

Chapter Ten

"How was class today?" Polly asked, a guilty expression on her flushed face. This was the first time in probably six years she had missed ballet, and the time before that was due to a bad case of the mumps.

"Fine." Jennifer nodded without looking up from her cheeseburger. "Balanchine's really going to be one of the judges at the school recital this year, believe it or not."

"Really? Madame's been trying to get him to do that for years," Polly said, taking another sip of coffee. The girls had met for a late lunch in the city after Polly had told Mme Mishkin that she wouldn't be in class for the next three weeks. As Jennifer had predicted, Madame had objected strenuously, although Polly was surprised when Madame had made a point of boasting to everyone in class that Polly had landed a professional job. On Bill Thompson, her opinion was considerably stronger: "Oh, that whoo-fer!" she had said disdainfully.

"Promises are one thing," Jennifer responded. "This time she has it in writing. And the best part is, the best dancer of the school—*if* one is picked this year—gets a formal audition for the City Ballet."

"You're kidding!" Polly gasped. "That's fabulous. Wouldn't it be something if you were selected! Oh, I hope it's you, Jen. You've improved so much this year. Also, you're a real Balanchine type—we've always said that."

Jennifer nodded dubiously. "I'm going to work my rear end off to get it." She took a small bite of her cheeseburger and chewed solemnly. "So, how was rehearsal?" she asked casually.

"It went pretty well this morning," Polly said, realizing that neither of them had even mentioned the possibility of her winning the school award or the audition. "I think I'm getting the hang of this hip twist thing."

"Watch out for your back. Remember that terrible summer you were lying around on a heating pad half the time?"

Polly smiled. She could see how concerned Jennifer was. She hadn't uttered one grouchy comment since Polly had accepted the part last week, as if she couldn't bear one more thing to come between them.

"You're right," she agreed, leaning her elbows on the coffee shop counter. "Any injuries now and I'm doomed. So much is going on in the next few months."

The girls were silent for a few minutes as the waitress refilled their coffee cups. Neither really wanted to say what was on her mind. Then, almost at the same instant, they both said, "The school recital's just around the corner."

They laughed and looked back into their cups, slightly embarrassed.

"I don't know if I'll be able to do it," Polly murmured.

"Not if you go to California, I guess," Jennifer bit her lip. She hated even to consider the idea, but it was there. "Madame started working on the group number today. She left a place for you in line. You should have seen Dawn making believe she was holding onto your arm. Boy, what a klutz!" Jennifer shook her head.

"Would you be very upset if I—"

"What?" Jennifer swiveled on her stool to face Polly.

"If I sort of changed course midstream," Polly said. "I mean, if all this works out."

Jennifer's intense face took on a determined look. "What's right for one of us isn't necessarily right for both, I guess. I think I've come around to that in the past couple of weeks. You know," she said, giving a quick laugh, "you like mangoes, and I like kiwis."

"You like starched shirt collars, and I loathe them," Polly added, grinning.

"You like Cott, and I like Andy."

"Hey, I thought you were giving Cott a chance these days."

"Oh sure, but you know what I mean. I don't turn all soft and blushy around him. I don't start panting when he walks into the room."

"I do not!" Polly said indignantly, both her eyebrows raised to their full height.

"Aw, come on. You do so." Jennifer chuckled, taking several dollars from her wallet to pay for her lunch. "You're so hooked that you're silly."

"Well, that's nothing new—the silliness, I mean," Polly said, laughing as she took her check over to the cashier. "We're both chronic cases."

"Maybe you are," Jennifer protested, "but not me! Serious me! I'm going to be a great ballerina and perform nightly to rave reviews and work my way up to soloist in two years!" she proclaimed.

"I bet you do it, too," Polly said softly as they paid and went to the front door. At first the thought of doing things differently from Jennifer had been painful, but now both of them were testing out the idea, preparing for the day when they might have to break apart, even for a little while. It was good to talk about it, even in this careful, guarded way.

"Tell me about Barry Newton," Jennifer pleaded as they strolled down the street. "Is he wonderful?"

"Well," Polly deliberated, "I wasn't crazy about him at first. Very vain, very much the leading man. I just can't stand it when he calls me cutie. I mean, look at me. Am I a cutie?"

Jennifer regarded Polly's elegant, well-turned out stance. "Positively not," she declared hotly, dragging Polly into Civic and Co., a boutique whose windows were always too appealing to pass by. "So did you tell him to stop?"

"Well, not exactly," Polly admitted, fingering a rack of designer jeans. "But I did ask him to bring me a cup of coffee when he went down to the canteen. He was so shocked! As you can well imagine, he is not the sort of guy to run errands. But, well, I was sweating my toes off, and he was just sitting around smoking those ridiculous brown cigarettes."

"Good for you." Jennifer picked up a white wool suit. "What about Shirley MacLaine?"

"Haven't met her yet, but I hear she's a doll. I don't get to do anything with her, so I probably won't even see her until dress rehearsal. Couldn't exactly have the Shirley of today bump into herself of twenty years ago."

"Wow!" Jennifer whirled, suddenly considering the possibility. "Wouldn't that be neat? To be able to contact your future self and find out what the next twenty years held in store. Then you'd be prepared for whatever lay ahead—like the recital and the scholarship and your show and Hollywood and—"

"Jennifer!" Polly exclaimed loudly, causing several shoppers to turn and stare. "Why are you so crazy about putting everything in little boxes? What would be the fun of going through life if you knew precisely what was going to happen? If I was certain about the Hollywood thing and knew that I'd have to give up the summer in Connecticut, I'd just be depressed. I'd rather have things hit me fast, like a shooting star falling to earth." Polly rammed one fist into an open palm to demonstrate.

"Do you think that's what's going to happen?" Jennifer asked in a small voice. "That you won't be able to take the scholarship?"

Polly sighed and looked at the floor. "Who knows? The answer is"—she paused for effect—"maybe—or maybe not!" Dragging Jennifer out into the cold again, she hurried her best friend along to the subway stop on the corner. No use in getting all worked up in a heavy discussion now. Certainly not before a nice evening with Cott.

"I'm walking over to Sutton Place," she said as Jennifer started down the steps to the subway. "Where are you and Andy going tonight?"

Jennifer rolled her eyes to the threatening clouds above them. "Where else? Another rock concert! That boy's ears can take more decibels than anyone else's I know. But it's REO Speedwagon, so I can't complain, can I?" She

grinned and bounced down the remaining steps.
"Bye!" she yelled over her shoulder.

"Bye," Polly called.

The Townsends were on their way to a friend's
club for the evening when Polly arrived. *I wonder if they ever just spend a quiet evening at
home,* Polly mused as she and Cott said goodbye to them at the door. Darya was all dressed
up in a shimmering gray silk top and black
evening pants with two silver stripes down each
leg. But gorgeous as she looked, she still seemed
awfully spacey to Polly. She couldn't carry on
the simplest conversation without fading out
after seconds. Polly couldn't imagine what an
intelligent businessman like Mitch Townsend
saw in his wife. *Well,* she thought as the door
closed behind them, *at least Mr. Townsend,
Jr., likes smart women.*

"What are you up for tonight?" Cott asked,
leaning back on the black leather sofa in the
den. He tugged her hand to pull her down beside
him.

"Hmm. I don't know—I'm too exhausted from
rehearsal to make sense. How about a movie?
Real escapist."

"Sure. You must be wiped out." He reached
over and massaged the back of her neck.

"Thanks, that's wonderful." Polly sighed, leaning into the pressure of his fingers. "Come to
think of it, I have been sort of beat constantly

for the past week. And this is just the dance part. The costume fittings and makeup sessions haven't even begun."

"What are you going to do about missing school?" Cott asked.

"Well, Mom went to the principal's office the day I got the part. She told all my teachers, and they all agreed to set up sort of individual tutoring stuff for the next three weeks if necessary. Jen's a great notetaker, so I really don't think I'll fall too far behind. The only real problem was Ms. Rosso, my science lab teacher. She said I'd fail the course because what I know about physics wouldn't fill an atom. Naturally, she's right."

"Aw, she's just jealous. Your physics are beautiful." He planted a kiss on the tip of her nose.

"Silly." Polly laughed, pushing him away. "So how about my movie?"

"Say, there's a Fred Astaire and Ginger Rogers retrospective across town. How about that?" He reached for her again and pulled her close. Polly rested her head on his shoulder. "That's perfect. Should we call for times?"

"In a minute." The shadows of the room grew longer as they sat together, fingertips touching. Polly could sense a pulse beating in her wrist. It was so strong that she knew Cott had to feel it, too. She kept thinking that it had been weeks and weeks since they'd really been alone together. Yet during that time, somehow, their relationship had grown and deepened. It was a combination of so many little things, like his new glasses—just for her—and his fierce determination that she get the part, even though he hated his father for butting in.

Polly rolled her head to the side and caught him watching her, a look of tender amusement on his still-tanned face.

"What?" she asked.

"Just looking at you, trying to capture the photograph in my head. You're—oh, Pol, you make me nuts!" He pulled her to him and held her tightly, their fingers still intertwined.

She remembered all the talks she and Jennifer had had over the years about guys and kissing and everything. The time, and the guy, had to be perfect. The whole thing had to feel as though it were destined, as though nothing else could possibly happen at that moment.

She retreated from his embrace slightly and smiled; then she bent forward to brush her lips against his. It was hardly a kiss, but she felt as if she were on fire. It was difficult to breathe, and yet, she felt so free, so relaxed. She wanted this moment to go on forever.

Cott began to stroke her hair gently, pushing the tousled auburn curls back from her forehead. "You won't really go to Hollywood if they ask you to?" It was almost a plea.

She sighed. "Don't let's talk about it. It's—it would be hard to say no."

"I suppose so," he admitted. "Say, this is really a laugh."

"What is?" Her hazel eyes held his gray ones in an intense gaze.

"You know. Here I move three thousand miles to Mamaroneck to meet the girl of my dreams, and my dear old dad sees to it that she takes my place back there. You'll probably even go to my old school, meet the guys I used to hang around with. Go out with one of them, even."

He got up and walked across the room, but Polly was right behind him. "Cott, don't be silly." Then she gave him a little shove and turned him around to face her. "I'm a one-man woman, and that's all there is to it."

"Oh, yeah?" He was wearing his I-don't-care look.

"Yeah," she said emphatically. "And nobody—not your father or Bill Thompson or any of the guys in your high school can change my mind about you. Underneath that cool California cucumber is the old-fashioned, nice Cott I know so well."

He took her hands in his. "Did I ever tell you how my nose got broken?" Polly had grown so used to his features she'd forgotten that his nose was slightly crooked, although it had been

162

one of the first things Jennifer had mentioned to her.

"No."

"Well, when I was at Beverly Hills High, I was with all these other celebrities' kids. Children of actors, producers, directors, stunt men, the whole deal. And it didn't matter how I really felt about my dad—I used to defend him all the time. Anybody who said anything about one of his specials got into a fight with me over it. Sometimes I even took a swipe at 'em if they said something good!"

Polly laughed and drew him back to his seat on the couch.

"Well, when I was a freshman, I was going with this girl, whose mother was a well-known actress. I wasn't that wild about her, but it was a status thing." He shrugged. "Looked good in the school paper gossip column. Anyhow, one day I turn up at the local burger shop, and there she is in a booth practically sitting on top of my best friend!"

"Oh, Cott!" Polly was filled with rage at the idea of anybody hurting Cott.

"So of course I picked a fight with the guy, and of course he was the better fighter, and I got my nose broken. It kind of healed the way your toe did."

"It looks fine to me," she said reassuringly.

"Well, the funny thing was that I didn't go

near another girl for three whole years. Then I moved here, and it was like starting fresh. A whole new beginning."

Polly exhaled sharply and moved into the circle of his arm. "I've never told you this, but I never really had a boyfriend either. Jennifer and I stuck to each other so much, I guess no guy wanted to even think about talking to one of us without the other. Let alone dating."

"But you knew when it was right." Cott grinned.

"You, too," she agreed.

They kissed again, this time very gently but longingly.

Suddenly, Cott moaned and pulled away. "Hey," he said softly, stroking one side of her face with his palm. "I'm crazy about you, but I'm not *that* crazy. We've got all the time in the world for this, Pol. Thanks to the magic of airplane travel," he added, wrenching himself away from her and getting up.

Polly frowned. "Think we better go see the movie, huh?"

"Exactly," he nodded emphatically, drawing her to her feet beside him.

They were almost at the hall closet before Polly could catch her breath again. How could she leave Cott for something as uncertain as the possibility of a part in a movie? She had never felt this way about anyone or anything before—as if part of her had taken root inside him and vice versa. Without actually understanding it, she just knew this was right. The two of them were meant for each other—it was as simple as that.

Chapter Eleven

Polly awoke with a start. It was still dark out, and the neon number of her radio alarm read 5:20. "Oh, no," she moaned, pulling the pillow over her head. She had been dreaming about the taping, and in the dream she was running down different corridors searching desperately for the right studio. If she could just find the lit red light, she would be fine—she remembered all her steps and everything. But then the monitors all along the hallway began running the credits for her show. She was nowhere near the right studio; she was going to miss her cue! That was the moment when her eyes flew open and she sat up in bed, her heart pounding.

"February thirteenth," she muttered to her pillow. "Today's the day."

Well, she was as ready as she'd ever be, despite the anxious nightmare. The weeks of rehearsal had given her a new sense of accomplishment about her dancing. Strange that throughout all those long years in ballet, she had never felt the sort of confidence she had when working with Bill Thompson. After the first few awkward rehearsals where her hips refused to get in line with her feet, she had mastered the jazz ballet almost effortlessly. Thompson, who had initially decided to choreograph something relatively easy for her, eventually changed his mind when he saw how fast she caught on, and piled one technical feat after another into a humorous but fluidly graceful routine. When she whipped through it in dress rehearsal without one mistake, even Mitchell Townsend had seemed impressed.

She flopped over on her back and stared at the ceiling. Now if she could just do it once more. And then she could go back to her normal life. Not that anyone could really consider it normal!

Polly laughed aloud as she thought of it. Like Cinderella the day after the ball, except that in this case, she might have to leave her Prince Charming. And if she left him, would she lose him, too? It was so unfair, really. The reward for doing well in the taping could turn out to be separation from Cott—and for how long?

"Oh, rats," Polly muttered to herself, swinging her legs out of bed. "Will you please just stop this craziness for a while!"

It was only ten of six by the time she'd taken

a shower and washed her hair, so she turned on her bedside lamp and tried going over the corrections on her French lesson. No good, she just couldn't concentrate. She picked up her trigonometry text, but that was even worse: the formulas and equations seemed to dance before her eyes. Finally she gave up, struggled into her leotard, and began such a strenuous floor warm-up that she was sweating in less than a minute. Then at seven-thirty she took another shower and went downstairs to the kitchen to start the coffee.

"Been up long?" asked Mrs. Luria when she walked into the kitchen several minutes later. She was already dressed in a beige corduroy suit, and she looked even more nervous than her daughter.

"Forever. I tried to go back to sleep, but my stomach was doing flip-flops on the mattress."

"I know, hon, but it'll be all over soon." Jane Luria came over to give Polly a hug and nearly knocked the coffeepot off the stove.

"You're not doing so well yourself, Mom." Polly laughed. "When can we go?"

"It would only make it worse to sit around the studio." She pressed Polly into a chair and began to make breakfast. "We'll just have a nice leisurely meal, and I'll drive you to school. You have, let's see"—she checked the clock—"nine hours to go until the taping."

"Oh, don't say it!" Polly doubled over and bur-

169

ied her head in her lap. "Maybe it won't happen. Maybe Shirley MacLaine will get sick." She pushed away the glass of orange juice her mother offered her. "No, please, I couldn't eat or drink a thing."

"You have to," her mother insisted, pushing it back. "The best thing you can do for yourself is to pretend this is just any other Friday—"

"Friday the thirteenth!" Polly interrupted.

"Just any other Friday the thirteenth, and you're going to do things the way you always do. Except for one thing."

"Aargh!" Polly yelped, jumping up and nearly knocking over the table. "The most important day of my life, mother, and you want me to eat meals and go to school!"

"Yeah, yeah," Jane Luria nodded unsympathetically. "And you told me only last month that the most important day of your life was when you met Cott."

"Oh, well, that's different." Polly blushed, rattling her coffee cup in its saucer.

"Love always is," her mother said, smiling.

"Mom!"

"Come on, sweetheart, you'll be late for school."

Polly dreamed through the day. Every once in a while, in the middle of English and math, she would work her feet furiously under her desk, marking the steps. Sometimes she would roll her head around on her neck to try to relax,

170

out it was useless. Even getting an A in the European history exam didn't snap her out of it, and when the final bell rang at three, Cott practically had to carry her downstairs to his waiting car. Her mother would be driving Jennifer into the city right after she saw her last client of the day.

"Polly! Sleeping Beauty! This is it!" Cott nearly shouted in her ear.

"It's hopeless," Polly told him miserably. "I'll never make it."

By the time they arrived at 30 Rockefeller Plaza, Polly was even more certain that she couldn't go on. They had stopped at three gas stations on the way in from Mamaroneck, and still her bladder protested. She felt the prickles of cold sweat on her forehead and the back of her neck. She had cramps in both legs and was starting to have some lower back pain. "What time is it?" she whispered to Cott as he half-pulled, half-dragged her from the MG in the parking garage around the corner.

"Exactly four-ten. You will be in your dressing room by four-fifteen. You are on time." He spoke very clearly, stroking her back as they walked along.

"God, I can't do this!" Polly bit her lip and looked at him with pleading eyes.

"What are you, chicken? Hey, you know the routine backwards and inside out. You look like a dream in your costume. You say your lines like a pro. What more do you want?"

"To have somebody else do it. To not be on trial. It's not like the rehearsals. Hundreds of people are going to be in the audience." They were now standing in front of the side doors of the building. People were streaming in and out past them.

"Hey, do you trust me?" Cott's gray eyes were filled with caring and tenderness. As Polly gazed into them, she felt like melting.

"Of course."

"Then just dance for me and nobody else. Pretend I'm the only one who's in the audience. Because, sweet girl, *I* am your biggest fan. First, last, and always."

Their hands touched and gripped before their lips met in a small, tentative kiss. Polly was suddenly warm all over. This kind, wonderful guy would protect her from the hard faces and criticism that lay ahead. Her boyfriend. She smiled for the first time that day.

"I'm ready," she said stoically.

"But the question is—is the *world* ready? Ready for the flying feet of Polly Luria!" Cott yelled, pulling her along.

The next hour was sheer agony. Polly was yanked away from a desperate Cott and taken firmly in hand by an assortment of costume mistresses, makeup designers, and hairdressers. Hardly anyone spoke to her—she was simly their rag doll to be pushed, molded, and shaped into whatever form they wanted. The only good thing about their merciless mauling was that it took Polly's mind off performing.

At last she was allowed to see the finished product in the mirror. She peered at herself as the last assistant took a final tuck in the shoulder of her costume and moved aside. She couldn't quite believe it—the image before her was sort of the Polly she knew, but not exactly. There was the tousled auburn wig blown out to look even fuller and more pixieish. No one who didn't know Polly would ever have suspected it wasn't her own hair. There were her deep brown eyes, painted with dramatic dance makeup in a variety of green-gold hues. Her rather white face had a dusting of glitter on her cheeks. Well, she was supposed to be a dream vision, after all, so the more abstract the better.

Her costume was ivory, covered with silver and gold sparkles. It was a variation on a plain leotard and tights—sleeveless with a V-neck and a small cape coming off one shoulder to drape down the back. Above the ivory tights, also sparkling, was a short wrap skirt with an uneven hem that stopped right at the top of her thighs. But what she liked best of all were the ivory ballet slippers. She had longed for a pair of white shoes for years, and her mother had always told her they were impractical and impossible to clean. Now, these would belong to her forever.

173

"Ten minutes, Polly," Sam shouted in the door and the panic immediately returned to her stomach. She got up and began a perfunctory warm up. Her feet didn't feel like they belonged to her.

Her mother and Jennifer were standing in the doorway when she turned around again. They were both smiling, Jennifer carrying a huge toy koala bear and Polly's mother a single red rose. Polly wanted to cry with happiness but she knew it would ruin her makeup.

"We'll be right out front," Jennifer promised. "Don't trip over the cables—and have fun!" Before Polly could call a thank you, they were gone.

"I'm back," said a deep voice right behind her. She turned to see Cott hidden behind an enormous bouquet of yellow roses. There must have been two dozen of them. "Are you okay?" he asked, squeezing her hand. "You sure look okay."

"Thanks," she said, blushing. "I'm—delirious I think. These are gorgeous." She breathed in their heady perfume.

"Polly," he said, placing the arrangement on the dressing table opposite her mirror, "I don't know how to say this. I've never said it before."

She saw the concern and embarrassment in his face. "What?" she asked softly.

"You know, it's this feeling I get when I look

174

at you. And then, when I go away from you, it's like everything hurts inside."

"Onstage for warm-up, Miss Luria." Sam stood there, unmoving, spoiling the moment. Polly and Cott just stared at each other, wishing they could be alone.

"I won't take my eyes off you. Remember—I'm the only audience." He walked with her and Sam to the end of the corridor, where Shirley MacLaine, dressed in the rehearsal clothes she would wear in the first scene, was talking intently with Bill Thompson.

"Good luck," Cott whispered before he disappeared through the big double doors. Polly could still feel his gaze on her, though, and it gave her the courage she needed to walk those last endless yards to the rehearsal room.

"Okay, gang," Sam called at 5:45 as Bill finished the warm-up. "We're taping in sequence. We get a good take, we go on to the next. You mess up, we stop and do it over. I don't have to tell you, time is money, so don't mess up. That's all."

Everyone wished each other good luck, Shirley MacLaine blew a kiss to Polly, and each actor and dancer took his or her place in the studio, some off camera. Those who weren't going on in the early segments went back to their dressing rooms. Polly stayed behind one of the cameras, flexing and pointing her feet, worrying about everything that might possibly go wrong.

Shirley MacLaine opened with a huge production number that went off without a mishap and led directly into her love song with Barry Newton. The audience went wild, and she acknowledged their applause gratefully.

Jim, the director, had obviously given the signal to go right on, so the crew quickly set up for the second segment. Polly felt dizzy as she took her place across the studio in the dream set. If this song went well, Shirley MacLaine would go into a remembrance about her early years as a dancer and the guy who gave her her first break, who, naturally, looked exactly like Barry Newton. That would be Polly's cue.

Where's Cott? she wondered miserably. *Why couldn't he signal or something?* She flopped over and bounced her head on her knees, trying to stay limber. In that moment, her brain spinning with hundreds of different thoughts, she realized for the first time why she cared so much about Cott. It was partly because he was warm and funny and smart and devastatingly handsome, but it was also because he appreciated Polly as Polly and nothing else. For as long as she could remember, people had lumped Jennifer and her together. If they liked Jennifer, they liked her, and vice versa. They were constantly tied together in people's minds. But Cott was crazy about her alone, no strings or other relationships attached. And that made Polly feel simply wonderful.

"You're up." Sam poked her in the ribs as the duet faded away. The audience was even more enthusiastic than it had been for the first number. Polly swallowed hard and quickly took her place in back of the prop door that a technician would open as soon as he got the cue in his headphones from Jim in the booth. Then, either Polly would start her routine or the world would come to an end. She didn't know which would be worse.

There it is. The door's open. Go! She stepped cautiously onto the set. The lights were even stronger than she had remembered from dress rehearsal.

"Cut!" The word boomed throughout the studio. *Oh God, what did I do?* Polly looked down at the white marks on the floor to see if she had already stepped out of bounds.

"What happened to the smoke machine?" Jim asked over the intercom. "I asked for dream smoke to flood the floor, then she walks into the middle of it."

"Sorry," called a technician. "We weren't ready."

"Polly, go back, we'll try it again. Apologies, dear." That was Mitch.

Her heart pounding, she moved back into place. If they stopped her again, she knew she'd never be able to do it.

The door opened on cue. This time there was plenty of smoke. Polly tried to ignore it and not cough as she stepped into the set. Was anything else going to happen? Did Barry make his costume change on time? Was that a real, live audience out there?

Don't think, just dance. Slowly, tentatively, just the way the character was supposed to. Polly explored the fake ballet studio, looking over her shoulder to be sure she was alone. The band struck up her theme, and she moved lightly from walking to dancing. It felt okay—as a matter of fact, it felt pretty good.

Barry entered for his part of the segment dressed similar to her in ivory, sparkling rehearsal clothes and a funny matching derby tilted over one eye. She said her lines; he answered. Then he was gone.

Polly wasn't really conscious of her body for the next four minutes. It was as if the steps were ingrained in her memory; she was carried on a wave of spontaneous power. Absolutely nothing passed through her mind—she was pure movement and feeling.

But when she concluded the number, she gradually became aware of a noise, thudding pounding, vibrating in her stomach. It was applause. They were applauding her. She straightened up and smiled, not sure what to do next. But when Sam hissed, "Take a bow," she did and the response was nothing less than phe nomenal. She curtsied a second time, then backed out the door into the waiting arms of Barry Newton. "Great, kid! You did it!" Someone took her hand and led her back to the dressing room. She felt numb and drained, but some small part of her was filled with a white-hot energy. She was ready to dance the entire night away with Cott, if he asked her.

It seemed like an hour before they let him back to see her, but once he was in the room, everything felt even better. "Congratulations," he said earnestly, wiping her dripping brow with her makeup towel. "Nobody'd ever seen anything like you before. Except me, of course." He shook her by both shoulders. "I'm so proud of you."

"I was dancing just for you," she said honestly.

"I know."

Then Sam came in and dragged them both into the control room so they could watch the rest of the taping. Shirley MacLaine was perfect, of course, and did everything splendidly with no need for retakes, but Polly was relieved when several of the chorus numbers had to be repeated because of mistakes. Her piece, thankfully, hadn't been the only do-over.

"Polly, I can't believe it." Jennifer ran into the booth, shrieking in her ear, jumping up and down. The second the show ended, she and Andy had bolted backstage.

"Darling, you were the best," Polly's mother

whispered when she could get close to her. "Your hair could have been neater, but I'm not complaining."

"Leave it to a mother to criticize." Polly mugged at Cott.

"It's only 'cause I love you," Mrs. Luria protested.

"Hey watch! They're rolling the credits," Andy said excitedly. All the monitors were lit up with the names of everyone responsible for the show, starting with Mitch and then MacLaine and Thompson. But after the first few big ones flashed on the screen, there it was. Polly's name, all by itself.

"I think I'll faint," Jennifer murmured as it went by. "She's my best friend! And she's on TV!"

Before Polly could recover her breath, she turned to greet a very pleased and smiling Mitchell Townsend.

"My dear," he said, taking both her hands, "you were superb. I can't tell you what an extraordinary performer you are."

"Thank you," Polly said shyly, suddenly feeling like shouting for joy because the whole ordeal was over.

"Thompson and I would like to get together with you sometime next week to talk about your future."

"Well, her future right now is a big fancy

dinner at Sardi's," Cott cut in, obviously eager to get away.

"When will I—? Do you have a broadcast date yet?" Polly asked.

Mitch shrugged. "It's set for mid-March right now. We'll keep you posted. See, the nice thing about videotape is you've forgotten all about the hard work by the time the show is on the air."

Forget it? Polly knew she never would. These steps, this part, this whole night would be with her forever. She had worked too hard to ever let it go.

"And then," Mitch concluded, "all you have to do is sit back and relax on the Friday night of the airing and watch yourself on TV."

Polly looked at him in mock disbelief. "Are you kidding?" She grinned mischievously. "And miss *Dallas!*"

Chapter Twelve

Polly had never known a month to seem so long. First she got word that the tape was cut and edited but that they had been bumped out of their time spot. Then Sam called and told her she could come in anytime for a private showing. But after thinking it over, she decided against that. She wanted to see it with the rest of America whenever it was scheduled.

A couple of weeks after the taping, she met with Mitch and Bill Thompson, and they told her how anxious they were for her to go to Hollywood for a screen test for the new David Stoneham movie, *Time-Step*. They had already sent a videotape of her segment to the producer and director, and they were waiting for a response. Much as the idea of a real Hollywood screen test thrilled her, Polly was hesitant. She couldn't imagine what it would be like, moving away from home and her mother and Jennifer. But the biggest wrench would be leaving Cott. She just didn't think she would be able to do it.

While going through the motions of school and ballet classes, she dreamed of the different paths her life could take. In one dream she went to California and became a famous actress overnight. In another, she went ahead and joined a ballet company with Jennifer. But the last dream, the most persistent one of all, had to do with Cott. She couldn't get him out of her mind. No matter that she saw him almost every day—he was still special. *Maybe this is what they mean by falling in love*, she told herself.

At last, late one afternoon, she got the call: April third was confirmed as the airing date. When the week finally arrived, Jennifer went out and bought a *TV Guide.* "Sometimes they list the whole cast," she insisted, flipping pages. But Polly's name wasn't mentioned.

"Maybe they cut my part out," Polly said anxiously.

"Dummy. They don't do that. Anyhow, you have a contract."

"I don't think I'm going to watch."

"You idiot! And spoil our party? You'd better."

Cott and Jennifer decorated the Luria house all Friday afternoon, while Joanne Taruskin baked up a storm. Jane Luria supervised the whole thing and set up a long buffet table on one side of the living room. Polly just bit her nails a lot.

At 8:30 sharp, the Taruskins, the Donahues, and the Lurias gathered around the TV. Cott held Polly's hand, Andy held Jennifer's, and the Taruskins stayed close to Jane Luria just in case she burst into tears.

Polly bit down hard on her lip as the first number began. Then the second one passed by, and she knew it was her turn. The camera shifted, and a billow of smoke filled the screen.

"Polly's on fire," Dr. Taruskin joked, but nobody laughed. The door of the set opened, and Polly stepped out, looking ravishing.

It seemed so unreal, so far away. Here she was, sitting in her own living room, surrounded by the people she loved best in the world, and yet, there she was inside that tiny box. And not just one box, but thousands, millions, across the country. There were more Pollys than she could begin to count, whirling and leaping and entertaining for all they were worth. But they weren't her; she was just a normal teenager glued to the tube on a Friday night, snuggled up close to her boyfriend.

"Wow, are you fantastic!" Jennifer breathed as soon as the piece was over.

"Pretty good, Polly," said Nancy Taruskin in her definitive manner. The parents were all talking on top of one another. Then the phone starting ringing, and the evening became total chaos. Aunts, cousins, even a second cousin from Los Angeles whom Polly had only met once, and friends from everywhere imaginable wanted to congratulate Polly. No one wanted to watch the rest of the show, and Dr. Taruskin seriously considered calling the station to ask them to repeat the segment.

Cott drew Polly into the kitchen, and they fussed with the food but were too excited to eat. "Let's drive to New York," Cott suggested. "We'll wait for the morning papers."

"Mom wouldn't let me, I'm sure," Polly protested. "Do you really think they'll review me?"

Just then the phone rang again, and Jennifer stuck her head in the door and nodded at her friend. "For you; who else? It's long distance."

Polly took the receiver as her mother tried to ply her with pretzels and chopped chicken liver. Polly giggled while she attempted to balance the plate and talk into the phone at the same time. "Hello?"

"Polly?" It was a man's voice, crackling over the bad connection. "I'm David Stoneham—maybe Mitch Townsend has mentioned my name?"

"Oh." Polly was instantly at attention. This was the director of the movie she was supposed to test for. "Hi, Mr. Stoneham."

"We've just seen your segment on the MacLaine show again, and we're extremely impressed,

Polly. I know from my talks with Mitch that you're still in school, but we'd like you out here by May first if you're interested in the part in *Time-Step*. Just say the word and we'll send you a ticket."

Polly looked at Cott, then at her mother and Jennifer. "When would I have to be in California?" she asked hesitantly, her eyes searching the faces of her friends for answers.

"We'd like you here by May first. I realize it means missing the end of your junior year, but we'll find a way for you to make that up."

"May first," Polly murmured. It was too soon. She just didn't want to tear herself away from this now.

"Do it!" said Cott to her amazement, squeezing her hand. Her mother's eyes were filled with tears, but she nodded her approval, as did Jennifer.

"I—I'm not sure," she said slowly into the phone. "I mean, I'd like a little time to think it over," she blurted out.

"Hmm. Well, we're anxious to get started, so if you can't get yourself out here, we'll have to go ahead with our number-two choice. We'd already picked the girl—but then you came along, see. Let me tell you again, Polly, how highly we think of you. Mitch and Bill have been talking you up to me for weeks, but I had to see for myself. The ticket's in the mail whenever you give the okay. But get in touch as soon as you can, Polly. We just can't wait too long."

"Thanks, Mr. Stoneham," Polly said after he had hung up. Then she turned to the assembled group, who were all suddenly silent. "I just don't know. It's such a big step." She shrugged. She didn't know what else to say, her mind was someplace else, back with those millions of Pollys, little pieces of her chipped off and crammed into TV sets across America, the fragmented Pollys who had just won her a chance at the big time. Could she really pass this up?

The *Times* was at the door as usual when she got up the next morning. With shaking fingers, she turned to the television page. There was a picture of Shirley MacLaine and a good-sized review of the show. Polly held her breath and began to read:

> The musical comedy special starring the irrepressible Shirley MacLaine was a treat for this reviewer. In her many years on the stage and in films, Miss MacLaine has become a symbol of feminine energy tempered with bittersweet appreciation of life experience. This hour and and a half special, produced by Mitchell Townsend and choreographed by Bill Thompson, was no exception.

Polly's eyes scanned the lines, not daring to hope. But then she gasped and sat down heavily on the nearest kitchen chair. The review continued:

> As Shirley MacLaine's younger self, newcomer Polly Luria was totally warm and believable. As well as being a brilliant technician, who can convey with movement more than most people can with words, she has all the poise of a far more experienced performer.

She read the words again and was just about to go over them a third time when Cott called. His father had early editions of the *Los Angeles Times*, the *Washington Post*, and the *Boston Globe*, as well as the daily *Variety*. Each review was more glowing than the other.

"This is just a fairy tale," Polly murmured, running her fingers over the *Times*, trying to make sure the words were still on the page. "I'll wake up tomorrow a frog again."

He laughed. "You were never a frog, kiddo. It's all happening."

"But it's—I don't know. It's not the real me."

"What do you mean? It's all you, Polly. It's your future if you grab it."

"Well," she said lamely, "I don't know that I want to grab it. Anyhow, why are you so excited about Hollywood all of a sudden? I thought you were desperate to keep me with you always."

Cott sighed. "Hey, let me be unselfish for once in my life, will you?" He paused, then he asked seriously, "What are you scared of, Pol? You've passed the hard part with high marks."

"Well, it's—" Polly stopped and looked around at the familiar kitchen. That clock, this table, that old tattered Baryshnikov poster her mother was always threatening to throw out. All of it was hers; it was home. "I can't imagine myself away from you and my mom and Jen."

"Maybe you won't have to be."

"What do you mean?"

"Well, my love, I just got some news of my own today. I got into UCLA."

Polly jumped out of her chair. "Oh, Cott, how fantastic! I'm so happy for you! We could both be in California then!"

"Wait a sec. I just realized something. If you start shooting in June sometime, you'll be through by the end of the summer. It's not the acting part of a movie that takes so long, Pol. It's the cutting and editing. You'll get your senior year at Mamaroneck High after all, give or take a few weeks. So you'd be back here when I was out there."

Polly stared at the phone glumly. "I should have known it was all working out too well," she murmured. "I don't think I want it anyway. I don't know."

"Yeah, well, that's the breaks. But look at the bright side, kid."

"What's that?" She sighed.

"I didn't tell you the other part of my news. Two days ago, I got another acceptance letter. I didn't want to steal your thunder, so I kept it to myself. I'm going to Columbia next fall. We'll be together right here, providing you don't get all starry-eyed about *Time-Step* and decide to stay in Hollywood to make a second film."

Polly was laughing so hard she couldn't even say congratulations. Now if she could only make up her mind about her own future. . . .

The dance recital took place, as always, in an old auditorium on the East Side that Madame Mishkin reserved every year. As Polly and Jennifer hurried along to the backstage door, they were both giddy and very silly. Polly didn't even feel a pang about not being in the recital—this was Jennifer's hour to shine.

"I just know you're going to be picked," Polly was saying as they swung the heavy backstage door open and the guard pointed them toward the dressing room.

"We are not going to discuss it," Jennifer said primly. "There may not even be a best dancer award this year. Balanchine may just be making this visit for nothing." Suddenly her eyes twinkled mischievously. "Oh, but if I win, Polly, I'll be so happy."

"Come on, time to make you beautiful. Here come the dazzling blue eyes, rosy pink cheeks, and the greatest hair you ever had." Polly plunked their makeup kit down on the dressing table and waved a perfunctory hello to the other girls whose mothers were nervously fussing over them. Dawn looked extremely self-confident as she pranced around the dressing room, already in costume and makeup, but Polly wasn't worried in the least. As far as she was concerned, there was only one candidate for this prize.

"Polly," Jennifer said, as her friend began serious work on her face, "this probably isn't the time to talk about it, and it's not my decision, of course, but you really ought to call that Mr. Stoneham back. You'll hate yourself forever if you don't give Hollywood a chance. I mean, you don't have to stay there. You could go, make one movie, and come home. Look at it this way—Robert Redford lives in Utah."

Polly jerked her hand away. "What's that got to do with anything?" She was all confused again about her options. It was fine when she didn't think about it, but impossible when she did.

Jennifer pouted at Polly's lack of comprehension. "Listen, if you get famous, you can live on the moon. But you'll never get famous if you don't take risks. Remember what you told me? Your life was going to be like a shooting star falling to earth."

Polly smiled and promised to think about it.

Here she'd always been the brave, independent one, and suddenly Jennifer was telling *her* to do something wild and different. When Madame came in half an hour later to begin the warm-up, Polly reluctantly said goodbye to her friend. "Remember to watch your turns," she cautioned, "and remember, this award is in the bag. All you have to do is claim it."

She joined Cott and Andy back at the box office. They had already directed the Taruskins to their seats and were waiting for her.

"Have you seen him yet?" she asked, jittery again but this time for her best friend. They handed their tickets to the usher and walked on through, down the aisle.

"Who?" said Andy.

"Who else?" Polly hissed. "Balanchine, of course." She found their row and slid in beside Joanne Taruskin. They exchanged nervous hellos.

"Hey, Pol," Cott said, patting her hand reassuringly, "he can't be bribed you know. If he likes her, he'll pick her."

Polly popped up again and craned her neck around, determined to get a glimpse of the great ballet master himself when he walked in. She tossed her head in annoyance at Cott. "You say it like it's so simple."

"Well, it is. You've been through this yourself, remember? Talent will out. You know that, I know that, and George Balanchine certainly knows it. And don't look now, but there he is."

Polly gasped, watching the great man stroll down the aisle accompanied by three colleagues— a man and two women—who looked like administrative types. And just at that moment, the lights dimmed, and the curtains parted.

Sixteen girls in color-coordinated tutus ranging from pale peach to deepest rose were standing in formation, their arms linked, their heads held high. Polly only saw Jennifer, wearing a warm mauve-colored costume, and she crossed her fingers as the taped music began. The group number was simple enough, but it was clear to Polly that no one could touch Jennifer's technique—the arch of her back, the line of her small body, the delicacy and strength of her movements.

A group of five dancers, including Dawn, took their places next and did a rather complicated, difficult piece. There wasn't a lot of feeling to it, but it looked flashy. Polly was getting worried, and Cott had to remind her to cool it, because Jennifer hadn't even appeared yet.

But she did more than appear in the next piece. She burst onstage as Titania in a segment from *A Midsummer Night's Dream* in which she is enchanted by Puck and falls in love with Bottom. Polly thought back to that English class so long ago when she had imagined the two of them as Helena and Hermia.

She wanted so badly for Jennifer's dream to come true—it was all she had wanted for as long as Polly had known her. Now, as queen of the fairies falling in love with a gawky, skinny Bottom (Alison Bean wearing a big donkey head), she was simply delightful. She managed to be pert and enticing while executing a lot of tough steps in rapid-fire succession. The girls dancing the other parts had to do their valiant best to keep up with her. The thing about Jennifer's performance that made it so exciting, though, was that she was totally into her part—she *was* Titania, and she was madly in love.

The audience was laughing with pleasure when the segment ended, and Polly noted that Balanchine was whispering animatedly to the people he'd come in with.

"Oh, God, she was so great!" Polly said to Jennifer's mother when they filed out for intermission.

"Yes, dear, I know that."

Andy was shaking his head in disbelief at his own reaction. "You know," he said, "I'm sort of getting to like this ballet stuff. I mean, it's not as bad as I used to think it was."

The second half of the program gave each girl a chance at a solo turn. Madame Mishkin was nothing if not fair. It seemed ages before Jennifer got onstage again, but when she danced the dying swan from *Swan Lake*, the audience sat spellbound. The amusing, perky Jennifer they had seen only a few minutes earlier was now the poignant, tragic ballerina. The contrast was astonishing.

Polly didn't really see much of the end of the program, and even the ensemble that ended the evening went right by her. She couldn't get over the fact that for all the years she'd known Jennifer, she had never really seen her at a distance. She had been so close to her for so long she'd never had the perspective to understand that Jennifer could do many different things well. *I wonder if she feels that way about me too,* Polly mused. She was now convinced that Jennifer had to win.

The judges took fifteen minutes after the applause had subsided to confer in a room back stage. Madame and Balanchine were on the panel, of course, as well as his colleagues and some of the teachers from the City Ballet School. There was one judge from Connecticut College and one from Juilliard, who would present the award.

When the decision had been reached, the curtains opened again to reveal the girls lined up in a semicircle against the back wall. The frozen expressions on their faces were testimony to the fact that each of them wanted this prize more than anything but each knew that there could only be one winner, if any.

The Juilliard representative took his place

enterstage and carefully pushed his large horn-rimmed glasses up on his nose. "Thank you for coming, ladies and gentlemen," he began. "I know it's been a great reward for all of us to see so much talent in one place at one time."

"Oh, get on with it!" Polly hissed under her breath.

The man talked for several minutes about Madame's school and the new young crop of professional ballet dancers who were coming out of it. Then he named at least a dozen famous alumni. Finally, he cleared his throat and announced that the judges had come to a final decision with great difficulty. "And so," he droned on, "we debated about giving three awards this year, instead of selecting the best dancer—an accolade, as you know, not often given."

"Oh, it can't be—oh, she has to get it," Polly moaned.

"But," he continued, propping up his glasses again, "we couldn't deny the fact that among these sixteen excellent dancers, one ballerina seems to have an edge, that certain something that stands out and promises a great deal for the future."

Polly was clawing the arms of her seat when the Juilliard teacher finally said, "It is with great pleasure that I now present the Best Dancer Award, as well as the certificate that goes with it. The winner of this very valuable award will, in addition, be asked to dance for the New York City Ballet with a possibility that she may be invited to join the company." He turned to the assembled girls behind him and smiled at each one. "We are presenting the award this year for the first time in five years. The title goes to Jennifer Taruskin."

Polly shrieked; Andy and Cott began applauding wildly. Mrs. Taruskin was crying on her husband's shoulder, and Nancy looked pleased. Jennifer, standing apart from the other girls, took the certificate with tentative fingers, as though it were a precious gem. "Oh, thank you," was all she could say. She took bow after bow—the audience wouldn't let her go.

Polly dragged the enthusiastic crew backstage and they were waiting in the wings when Jennifer at last staggered off. She looked totally dazed.

"Oh, Jennifer," her mother cried.

"Congratulations." Cott smiled as Andy took Jennifer in his arms and gave her a big bear hug. She looked right past them at Polly, who was in tears.

"I knew it," Polly said, moving closer to embrace her friend. "You had to win. Fate had to strike both of us at once."

"It looks like it." Jennifer nodded happily. "Different paths for each of us—but both good ones."

"Can I have her back?" Andy cut in, draping an arm around Jennifer's shoulders. "Hey, Jen," he said to her, beaming with pride, "you're turning me into a real balletomaniac!"

"That's great, Andy." She laughed. "It's nice to have the right kind of maniac behind me." And when she kissed him, Polly could tell that she really meant it.

Chapter Thirteen

"Where do you want these?" Jennifer asked, holding up a handful of leotards and bathing suits.

"The big suitcase, I guess. Just tuck them around the sides." Polly was standing in the midst of total chaos. Her bedroom had been torn apart in a mad attempt to pack everything it contained into two suitcases and a flight bag. Jennifer kept telling her it was impossible, but it was futile to reason with Polly now. Her plane for Hollywood was leaving in three hours.

"Well, you can't take George." Jennifer laughed, pointing to the koala bear, named for Balanchine, which was sitting at the head of Polly's bed.

"I guess George should stay," Polly reluctantly agreed. "Maybe you better take him to your house so he doesn't get lonely."

"Okay," Jennifer said. "I'll teach him one of

Madame's routines. You won't recognize him when you come home." She patted the bear's fat stomach.

At the mention of the word home, Polly was immediately anxious once again. Had she made the right decision? There was just no way of knowing.

"Do you have your own room at Barbara's?" Jennifer asked, pressing two cotton sweaters into the already bulging suitcase.

"Yes. It was awfully nice of her to let me spend the summer with her. After all, she's Mom's second cousin—it's not like they've ever been bosom buddies or anything."

"Yes, but she saw you on TV," Jennifer reminded her. "She's thrilled to have an honest-to-goodness celebrity living in her very own house."

Polly sat down heavily on the bed. "Celebrity, ha!"

Jennifer settled herself on the other end of the bed, shoving George aside to make room. "You will be," she said softly. "Hey, you never told me what made you change your mind."

"About going?" Polly looked thoughtfully at the tree just outside her window. New light-green spring buds were clearly visible. "Well, I made a list—the way you always do it. On one side I had negatives. Those were: leaving Cott, leaving you, leaving Mom, not finishing junior year, giving up the Connecticut College scholarship, going to a strange place where I don't know a soul—"

"Hey," Jennifer said, laughing, "this list must have run off the page! What was on the plus side?"

"Having an adventure." Polly's hazel eyes took on a dreamy, mysterious look. "Being brave enough to try something I'm not sure I can do. And getting in a movie," she added, almost as an afterthought.

"Well, I'm glad."

"I *think* I'm glad."

The girls looked at each other, then quietly went back to the mammoth chore of packing.

"Polly!" yelled Mrs. Luria up the stairs. "There will be inspection before Cott drives you off to the friendly skies of United. That room had better be spick-and-span."

"Yes, Mom," Polly called back. To Jennifer she commented, "She watches too many commercials."

Dissolving in giggles, the girls began straightening up the mess they had created, setting aside "vital" items to be crammed into the suitcases, placing others back in drawers and into the closet.

Suddenly Polly glanced down at her watch and gasped. "Oh, my God, I'm really doing this!"

"Of course you are," Jennifer said sensibly.

"But suppose—what if I've made the wrong choice? At least you know you're an expert ballet dancer—you have the certificate to prove it and everything. You have your scholarship, so you get to spend the summer sharpening up the skills you already have." She sat on the bed again and sighed deeply. "But I'm just a novice at this film stuff. Suppose I'm terrible? Suppose I die of homesickness? Suppose I hate California?"

Jennifer took her frantic friend by the shoulders. "Look, you can always come back, right?"

Polly's voice suddenly got all choked up. "What, and admit failure?"

"To me you can," Jennifer said simply. "What are best friends for, anyway? Now," she continued, going back to work, "what else has to be packed?" She lifted Polly's ivory ballet slippers from their peg on the wall and deftly tucked them into the one remaining space left in the second suitcase.

"For luck," she whispered.

"For luck," Polly repeated.

Cott was early, but everyone was ready long before it was time to leave for the airport. Mrs. Luria hastily put supper on the kitchen table, but nobody was very hungry.

"What time did you tell Barbara to pick you up?" Mrs. Luria asked anxiously.

"The plane gets in at eight-thirty L.A. time, Mom. That's eleven-thirty here," Polly reminded her.

"I'll change all the clocks for the next three months," Jane Luria promised her daughter. Then, as she dished out the hot dogs and coleslaw onto four plates, she wailed, "Oh, no, my baby is going away!"

Jennifer squeezed her hand. "It's not for long," she assured her.

Polly was holding back tears, and Cott was making a real effort to eat, since no one else was. There was silence for several minutes, then everyone spoke at once.

"Great coleslaw, Mrs. Luria," Cott declared.

"I wish this wasn't happening," said Jennifer while Polly slapped one hand to her head. "Mom, I left my winter coat at the cleaner's. Could you pick it up for me, please? Oh, where'd I put the ticket?"

Then Mrs. Luria started crying, and the meal was over.

"We better start packing the car, don't you think?" Cott suggested softly to Polly. "It's getting to be that time."

"You're right. The bags are sitting in the hall. Just let me run upstairs and check to see whether I've forgotten anything."

As the others took her things out to the Toyota (the MG was too small for the luggage), Polly wandered upstairs. She touched the banister and felt the smooth, polished wood. She rubbed it like a good-luck charm, praying it would bring her home soon. Down-to-earth as she was about most things, she sort of believed in these little rituals—just the way she had been sure that a magic bottle of suntan lotion would help her get a part in a TV special.

She walked the last few steps to her bedroom and scanned each corner, each piece of furniture. Everything looked just as it always had—a typical teenager's room with its flowered print wallpaper and Danish modern desk and chair, the twin bed and the small brass lamp on the bedside table. It was her world. But not her whole world.

She swallowed the lump in her throat and walked down to the car, grabbing her purse and trench coat off the hall table. Cott was leaning on the Toyota, trying to joke with Jennifer and Mrs. Luria, but he didn't seem to be getting much response.

"Everyone ready?" Polly said with a brightness she didn't feel.

"Polly, hon, you know how I am about airports." Her mother, now dry-eyed, shook her head. "I'd rather say goodbye here." Polly threw out her arms and embraced her mother, nodding her understanding.

"I'll call as soon as I get to Barbara's, okay?"

Her mother stepped back, just a little closer to the house, and Cott climbed in behind the wheel.

"I'm not going either, Pol," Jennifer said in a small voice. "I couldn't stand it. You better write every single day, and if you run into Brooke Shields, you can tell her for me I don't think she's as marvelous as she's cracked up to be."

The girls flung themselves together, hugging each other tightly for several minutes. "Take care of yourself," Jennifer said, drawing away. "I won't be around to keep you on track."

"Yeah," Polly agreed. "And I won't be here to keep you from languishing in utter seriousness."

She walked around to the passenger side and climbed in, feeling as if every motion she made brought her closer to the end. Cott started up the engine and began edging slowly down the drive, but Polly reached out and grabbed Jennifer's hand once more. "I'm coming home in a blaze of glory," she promised.

"You'd better," Jennifer cried, and then Cott gunned the engine. Polly waved madly at her mother and her best friend until they were out of sight. Then she sat back and watched the streets and stores and signs whiz by. She was being taken swiftly away from everything she was used to. She had never been away from home alone before.

"How're you doing?" Cott asked, turning onto the highway.

"Okay. Not great. Lots of butterflies doing *The Rite of Spring* in my stomach."

"You'll be better when you get on the plane and they close the door behind you." He grinned. "Then there'll be no escape."

Polly sighed and leaned toward him. "What about you? What's the game plan for this summer?"

"Well, I hate to tell you, but Dad's pretty set on Europe. He's going to grab up a lot of international talent and bottle it, I think."

"Oh." Why was Cott suddenly so calm, as if he didn't care if she left or not? Why didn't he say something to make it all right?

"I'll try to get out to the Coast to see you before we leave, but it looks iffy right now." The Toyota sped across the bridge, and in a few minutes they saw the first signs for the New York airports. Polly felt miserable. This wasn't the way it was supposed to be. So cold and unromantic. "Then she heard him say, "I don't know how I'm going to stand it—being away from you. It could be till September. I'm going to run up a huge phone bill, calling you from Eastern Bavaria or someplace."

She glanced over at him and saw bright tears brimming in his eyes.

"We can make it," she said. And at that moment, she knew that they could.

In no time they were driving down the road at Kennedy Airport toward the United terminal. Cott swung into the nearest parking lot and took Polly's two large suitcases out of the back.

She carried her flight bag, trench coat, and purse.

Walking as close to one another as they could, they approached the United doors, which automatically zoomed apart as soon as they stepped on the mats.

"May I help you?" asked a uniformed check-in clerk with a plastic smile.

Polly took her ticket out of her bag and passed it to the woman while Cott lifted her suitcases onto the conveyor belt to be tagged. She answered the routine questions about nonsmoking and window seat in a dull, listless voice.

"The eight-thirty to Los Angeles is boarding at Gate Seventeen B," the attendant said cheerily. "You'd better hurry along now. They're on time."

"Just our luck," Polly muttered under her breath as they walked away, down the corridor to the gates. She felt awful. There was so much to say to him, and no time to even begin.

Cott grabbed her hand and began hurrying her along. "Wait. We have to do something first."

Polly clutched her flying belongings to her chest and tried to keep up with him. "Where are we? . . . What's going on, Cott?"

"This is important." He put one hand on the small of her back to steer her along faster. "You're not leaving without one." There was an impish look in his eyes that somehow managed to cheer Polly up just a little.

"Now," he said when they reached a gift shop, "just wait here. Don't go away." He raced inside and spent several minutes deep in conversation with the cashier. When he finally emerged from the shop, he was carrying a small brown paper bag. "For you—forever," he whispered, placing it in her hands. The object was hard and round. Polly looked at him, puzzled, and drew it out of the bag. When she saw it, she smiled, then reached over to kiss him on the cheek. It was a paperweight. Inside the glass ball was a picture of the Empire State and Chrysler buildings, surrounded by a lot of Manhattan hubbub and tiny figures scurrying around through busy streets. Above the skyline were the words, Greetings from New York. When she shook it, snow swirled around the city scene.

"Thank you, I love it," she said, hugging it to her.

"Yeah, well you're gonna *need* it when you see all that California sunshine." He made a face. "Guess we better get you on that plane."

"Guess so."

They walked to the gate in silence. Other passengers were already boarding the plane. Polly looked up at Cott, hoping he'd hold her, tell her not to go. Instead, he led her over to the big plate-glass window where they could stare out at the huge gray machine that would soon be taking Polly three thousand miles away.

"I'm going to miss you so much," Cott said, taking her in his arms. "I think about you all the time as it is."

"Me, too," she agreed. "About you. Oh, I hate goodbyes." She threw her arms around his neck and nestled her cheek against his.

"They're lousy. But think how good our hello is going to be. Hey," he said, drawing away so he could look into her eyes, "I have to let you go do your own thing. You deserve that. And you don't have to worry. I'll keep a candle burning in the window for you."

"How old-fashioned."

"That's me. Just an old-fashioned California guy, in love with a gorgeous New York girl."

They looked at each other, and the last call for boarding boomed over the loudspeaker. Polly felt it thudding inside her chest. "I have to go."

He bent down and kissed her gently, folding his arms around her slim form, drawing her as close as he could. After a long moment, she pulled away reluctantly, and they walked together toward the door.

"I'll call you at Barbara's at nine California time," he promised, not letting go of her hand.

"I'll be waiting by the phone." She jerked her hand away and turned so she wouldn't see him, then ran down the ramp into the plane. The stewardess took her boarding pass, and she marched determinedly ahead to find her seat. *I don't want to leave him*, she thought as she peered out the tiny window. *But I am.*

There was Cott in the terminal, standing at the big window beside the gate, waving madly at her plane, his eyes searching for her everywhere.

"Oh, I'm here!" she said softly, almost in tears because she knew he couldn't see her.

The seat belt and no-smoking signs were on now; the flight personnel were already getting their oxygen masks ready for the demonstration.

Polly sat gripping the sides of the little window, willing Cott to know she was there, right before his eyes. She thought of New Year's, and of lunch in the Promenade Cafe, and of Cott and Jennifer making coffee together on Thanksgiving night.

As the plane began rolling down the runway, she took a breath and swallowed the sadness threatening to overcome her. After all, she was going off to a new life in a new city. There were hundreds of things to think about.

But then she called up Cott's handsome face, no longer visible except in her mind, and she smiled. She thought of him kissing her, holding her. If it hadn't been for him, none of this would have happened. So he was part of her new life—she wasn't alone. Tucked away, deep inside her heart, he was traveling with her. And when they saw each other again, a month from now or three months from now, the feelings would still be there, undimmed by time or distance, as strong as ever.

The air pressure in the cabin pushed down on Polly as the plane lifted into the air. She pushed back, sitting upright in her seat. Whatever happened now, she was ready.

Read these great new
Sweet Dreams romances

of lies and confusion—until the night when her lies go too far.

#17   ASK ANNIE by Suzanne Rand

At first, Annie was thrilled to give Tim advice about his girlfriend—until he asks Annie how to keep beautiful, stuck-up Marcy in line. If she helps Tim keep Marcy, Annie will never get a chance with him. But if she doesn't, will Tim stop being her friend?

#18   TEN-BOY SUMMER by Janet Quin-Harkin

Jill's vacation gets off to a wild start when her best friend, Toni, thinks up a contest—who can be the first to date ten new boys! It seems like a great idea until Jill meets Craig and knows she's in love. If Jill drops out of the contest, she won't be able to face her best friend. If she doesn't, she'll lose Craig forever.

And make sure to look for these Sweet Dreams romances, coming soon: